I0718251

THE BEAST

BOOK VIII

JP ROSSELLE

Copyright © 2023 by JP Rosselle.

ISBN   978-1-953821-68-3 Ebook
ISBN   978-1-953821-67-6 Paperback

All rights reserved. No part of this publication may be reproduced, distributed, or transmitted in any form or by any means, including photocopying, recording, or other electronic or mechanical methods without the prior written permission of the publisher. For permission requests, solicit the publisher via the address below through mail or email with the subject line "Attention: Publication Permission".

This is a work of fiction. Names, characters, places and incidents either are products of the author's imagination or are used fictitiously.

The EC Publishing LLC books may be ordered
through booksellers or by contacting:

EC Publishing LLC
116 South Magnolia Ave.
Suite 3, Unit F
Ocala, FL 34471, USA
Direct Line: +1 (352) 644-6538
Fax: +1 (800) 483-1813
http://www.ecpublishingllc.com/

Ordering Information:
Quantity sales. Special discounts are available on quantity purchases by corporations, associations, and others. For details, contact the publisher at the address above.

Printed in the United States of America

Table of Contents

CHAPTER I

OUR WAR ON DRUGS

It was after 11:00 p.m. when I retrieved my guns and exited the White House, I went right to the airport where Tommy was waiting with the leer. We took off and I was back in Miami by 4:00 a.m. When I opened the apartment door Lori was sitting on the couch watching TV. She ran and kissed me saying she wasn't worried about me, she just couldn't sleep. We got our hot shower and went to bed. The next morning, Lori didn't make it to school on time. She would need the sleep as today would be her last swim meet before State's.

I had walked down and picked up the Morning news, I didn't blame him, but Tim hadn't given us very much heads up on the photo. The photo that was printed wasn't the same photo Tim had given me, but it did have Gonzales in the same room as the President. The information about campaign money coming from Gonzales was also printed.

Lourdes called and said the Secretary of State had called asking me to return his call. I was hesitant as I knew he was going to say he told me so. I would wait until Lori left the room then I would return his call. Before I could call him back, Tim called my cell phone. News paper Tim said that less than 15 minutes ago Gonzales's bank had been raided by the FBI and DEA and that early this morning Gonzales had been arrested at his home on Starr Island. Tim said he was present at both happenings. Tim was calling me to thank me for the heads up as he said that he was called and tipped off 30 minutes before the arrest. Tim said that no other news people were at the scene, it was an exclusive. I didn't take the credit but mentioned that he should go light on the President. Tim said that he had also received a response from the White House that Gonzales had been an unsolicited contributor to the Presidents campaign and that the monies had be returned. Tim said he was sorry he couldn't thank me in person because he would be quite busy with the ongoing story. As I hung up I called for the Secretary, the Secretary then called back and without saying much, he apologized saying that I was on the right track. He ended the phone call saying that we should keep in contact and hoped we would meet again soon. Neither of us mentioned anything about Gonzales.

As I walked back in from the balcony Lori was coming to kiss me good-bye. She reminded me that Saturday was modeling day. I said that I had forgotten and that if ok with her, I would send for Christina to go along with her and Lilly as I would be going to Nassau for two days. Lori said that would be fine and that if ok, she wanted to visit the beach house on Nassau Saturday after the photo ops. Lori said that Angee was going to show her how to cook some of my favorite dishes. I told her I would be spending some time with Salinas and the children. Lori said she knew as she and Salinas had talked. Lori said that Salinas said that she had also talked to Christina and was all caught up with Christina's plans.

My kiss from Lori was so good that I wished that Lori didn't have school today. She was late to school and was having her last regular swim meet after school. Lori might not have yet heard the news of the sailing club shooting and I hoped she would not. Seemed like more time had passed but it was only yesterday.

In checking Lourdes's messages, Montibelli had called along with Malcolm. I first called Malcolm, Malcolm had been speaking with Lori and first congratulated me on our marriage. Malcom knew he had lost the school year but wasn't ready to return to Miami. Malcolm asked if I had work for him in Nassau. Yes, Malcolm wanted to work on one of the crawfish boats. Malcolm said of course; his Mom wanted him to stay put. Malcolm said he wanted to come to Miami this weekend but wanted to check if he could still be friends with Lori. I laughed and said that it would make me happy to have him as one of the family. Malcolm thanked me for all the assistance with Roy and the new car. Malcolm said he wasn't ready to get behind the wheel again. I offered to send Tommy for him, but Malcolm said he would be on a United flight, tonight. Malcolm said that Lori had offered to pick him up at Miami International. It was great hearing from Malcolm; as I walked out on the balcony, I thought of his father, Carson. It then hit me that I didn't have a friend, I had the girls, but if I just wanted to take off and go somewhere it would be by myself. I missed Carson.

I called Montibelli and we lunched, Montibelli said that the people of Iran and the free world thanked me. I asked him what he knew of the free world? Well he said, for the moment we know that there's someone out there that has the balls to do something about the suffering. I looked at him and said that we both were making money from people suffering. Montibelli asked permission to deliver Lori a new car, a gift he said. I thanked him but declined, no I said, that part of her high school will stay put. That part meaning the Jeep.

Montibelli had heard about the sailing club thing and said that the man that had escaped had been located in Columbia and punished. The man that sent him, Montibelli said was, at the moment untouchable. Montibelli was talking about Pablo Escobar. Escobar, Montibelli said had better protection than the US President. Montibelli said that a mental cripple had gotten to the President. Montibelli said that Escobar would probably outlive us all.

It was time to go to the pool. When I walked in, Lori was warming up, she saw me and came a running, she was crying saying that one of her friends had told her of yesterday's events. Settle down I said, everything is just fine, no one was after me. I can't lose you she said, I can't, I won't. I'm not going anywhere I said I'm right here. Now I said go on and show me what you got. I kissed her and turned her around and gave a small push. Lori turned and said we're not finished with this conversation.

Lori didn't do her best during the meet. For the first time, she had come in second in her 50-meter free style. The team's senior came in first with Lori a close second. The 200-meter relay went much the same with Lori not giving her teammates that normal commanding win. They did however win the relay and the meet. The team would now have two weeks to prepare for States. Lori's Coach asked that I please have our home life straightened out before then. Our home life I thought. Lori's teammates went out to celebrate the winning season, Lori and I went home to a hot shower and bed.

Lori asked if she could go and pick up Malcolm from the airport. She asked about missing school the next day to spend the day with Malcolm. I said there'd be plenty of time for socializing with Malcolm, and I didn't want her missing school. Lori left the house at about 9:00 p.m. and returned with Malcolm. It was a pleasant surprise to see Malcolm. Malcolm was frail looking, maybe down 30 or so pounds. Although there was a larger brand new BMW in his driveway. Lori said that Malcolm said he wasn't ready to do any driving. They hadn't stopped at Malcolm's house; they had come straight here. I called Malcolm's house to let his house woman know not to wait up for him. Malcolm had a sealed letter that his mom had written to give me. I walked into the bedroom and opened the letter. The letter was short and not so sweet; it said she was against Malcolm coming back to Miami. Malcolm, she stated, was still having trouble sleeping and eating and still got headaches. She added that he has not recovered from his accident and needed a mother's care. I walked into the bathroom and threw the letter in the round file. I thought to myself, what Malcolm needed was some good old salt air. I only walked back out to stay good night, noting that for Lori, it was a school night.

The next morning Lori got off to school, but before she left, she asked that I stay for her Saturday's photo shoot and that we all go to Nassau together. Together you mean Malcolm too, I asked? Lori said yes. I said I'd think about it and let her know.

Malcolm was up early and sat out on the balcony with me, drinking coffee. He and I mapped out what he was going to do. He would travel with us to Nassau and start working the crawfish boats and train with Christina and Maria. I would stay the day, tomorrow going to Lori's and Christina's photo shoot, then us all going to Nassau.

That afternoon Christina and Maria came in, and we all would catch a movie and go out to dinner.

The next morning, we all got an early start, the photo shoot didn't start until 10:00 a.m., we all met down at the sailing club. From there we all took out the Morgan. The boat was full of personal. But I thought that the idea of Mrs. Shinner was a good one. I could tell the photos of the two girls behind the sailboat's wheel were going to be home runs. Both girls were asked to remove the rings that they were wearing. Lori's wedding rings on her finger and Christina's ring on her finger and the ones she wore around her neck.

It was a gorgeous day out on Biscayne Bay. Big Ted had his work cut out for him today, them having two security boats out there with us. It seemed that a boat load of camera people drew some attention, not to mention the girls. Several onlookers were flagged off from getting too close. I could tell that the girls when Mrs. Shinner was finished would have been happy just to drop the camera people off at the dock and head right on back out to the ocean. This wasn't to be as I was already late for a date.

Malcolm and his house women would accompany us to Nassau. Malcom would be moving into my old apartment while Ms. Sandy, the woman we hired for Malcolm's Miami house, would stay at her own house in Nassau. At the Nassau airport, I told Lori that she was to be back at the airport tomorrow at 6:00 p.m. where Tommy would fly her home. I kissed her and said I'd see her in a few days. I jumped in a taxi and headed to the Hill Top Beach House.

I hadn't seen Salinas and the children in almost a month. Wendy Michelle, Johnny, Michelle, Kelly, Jimmy and Jacques were our six children. Everyone was dress and waiting my arrival, what a show. Salinas was wearing an Island dress that was blue in color with three different colored hibiscus flowers on it. I couldn't see much of her shape, I was anxious to get her alone but it wasn't to be. Looked like all these kids were trained to say, Papa. Papa, Papa, even the little ones who were barely walking or not walking at all had their arms out for me. From there it was to the beach. It was like Salinas had seen Lori's Burdines modeling adds as she was wearing that one piece black bathing suit. Wow did she look good, no not good, great! I realized that Salinas had quite some time to plan all of this, right down to keeping her distance from me so I could watch her moving with the kids, picking them up and running in and out of the water with them. It was strange that all of them kept looking at me. Another thing I noticed that there was more help. Seemed that Salinas had good taste in hiring help. It was hard not to notice. I thought it strange that Salinas would hire anyone that looked like that in a bathing suit, not one but two of them. Even the bathing suits they wore could have been a bit more conservative.

From the beach, it was to the pool and from the pool it was nap time. Yes, a nap for Salinas and me too. It was a great hot shower and then to bed. Salinas had regained about 90% of her old body back. She said the other 10% was on the way. Salinas for the first time had her local Doctor put in one of those "Ts" that we had always talked about. I was reminded that her and Christina had made a pack that Christina would bare my next child. Salinas asked if that had now changed and if Lori would now have my next child? I confirmed that my relation with Christina had changed and that there were no plans for Lori to have any children for quite some years to come. Salinas said she would be ready to have as many more as I wanted. I said that she'd be taking a break from having children so she could travel with me starting in September. Salinas asked where we would be going? I told her that we would be building an airport at her home town of Port a Paix. Your not sending me home are you she asked? No I won't be sending you anywhere without me I said. I told her that we would be making Paix our most southern air hub. She asked about Andros and I told her that we would still have presents there but, no cargo unless coming in or out of the Bahamas. I told Salinas that within the next few weeks she and I would revisit General Namphy whom was still in charge of Haiti. We were going to buy the Paxi airport and all the land from there to the Chateau. She asked whom would be the owners of such a place? I said you and the children. Salinas said the dirt in Paix was fertile and could grow anything, even bananas. My reply was that we'd see about that. Getting reacquainted with Salinas in bed was quite something.

The next day was much the same as the day before with playing with the children. I did get up early enough to go and visit Mark at the fishing boats. This Sunday only two boats would be going out to pull traps. Mark would have been having the day off too except I had sent word I would be visiting the dock. It was great to see Mark and the men. Otis's and his boat were missing from the dock but Mark said that the "JOHNNY" was in the shop for a make-over and Otis would be going to church with the family. Mark and I talked a short time about the crawfish and then I talked about Malcolm. Malcolm was to start tomorrow going out in the same boat as Mark or Mary's husband Tim; yes, Tim had worked his way up to captain.

Angee wouldn't be at work today as she would be going to church with Otis and Maggie and then giving a cooking class to Lori. Me I headed back home as Betty said she was a cooking up some of her famous pancakes. My how I missed Betty's good food.

Seemed that all of us at the Hill Top House would be eating breakfast together. The table in the kitchen seated 12 and there were ten of us sitting for pancakes. Yes, the two girls that Salinas had working with the children would also be seated with us. Salinas had said the night before that these girls were not Bahamians but Haitians. Salinas said all our children would speak the Queens English and French. Both girls that Salinas had picked to help with our children were girls whom were living at the Paix Chateau as family of our Haitian Militia.

Lori had departed Nassau to return to Miami while Christina and Maria stayed. Angee had started the cooking class and sent one of her restaurant cooks with Lori to Miami to continue the classes. I thought this a great idea to not have Lori at home alone.

Salinas and I would dine tonight at the Bahamian Cuisine restaurant. Tomorrow we would take Donzi to Harbor Island, have dinner at the Pink Sands hotel and then spend the night at our house there. Salinas dressed for both dinners, I didn't have any idea where those dresses had come from but wow! That flowered dress from Saturday didn't show any of her curves but the one from last night and tonight made it so that I couldn't take my eyes off her even if I had wanted too. I asked where the dresses had come from and she calmly said Paris. Oh yes, tonight's dress was worn without shoes.

Salinas and I stayed for two more days then headed back to Nassau. I hadn't had any news and thought that Lourdes was just giving me a break.

Once in Nassau the news from Lourdes was that the new CIA chief had called and asked to visit. I thought he meant Andros but he wanted to come to Nassau. He would fly in the next afternoon and we would go fishing. No not that kind of fishing, real fishing. We actually did fish and we did catch some good ones. The Director being the same age as my father told me of his start as a lawyer having the Vietnam War interrupt his practice, him becoming a Naval officer during the war then after the war, into public service as a judge then the FBI Director with the peanut President, then the CIA and now heading up the same for our present President. The Director said he was aware of me since 1978 when, I was thought to have been connected with the mob. He remembered Benny well, the Director said he liked how I had gotten Jena out of the house the day of her father's funeral. He was talking about Benny's house the day after Benny had died. The Director said he had a man on the inside and his man was at the house that day. The Director said Guido sure was mad. He said they didn't know that I had owned the property of the casino on Paradise Island until I sold it right from under Guido's big feet. He said they had heard many stories about me to including my 1974 trip to Cuba, rescuing Carson from Angola in 1975 and seeking Carson out in Grenada in 1983. The Director said he was sorry about Carson and if I remembered, he was the one that had talked at Carson's funeral. He said that they all had figured that I had done away with the King Fish and was satisfied how it ended up. He asked if I had kept up with the Senator? Died a terrible death, found behind the wheel of his demolished car I said. The Director said yes. I said the Senator most likely didn't feel a thing or was already dead. The Director said, you don't trust anyone do you. I said that only one disciple wasn't a fisherman.

The next morning when exiting the boat, Salinas was there waiting for us. As many Bahamian women did, Salinas had her hair up in a bun and was now wearing a typical Bahamian dress. The Director said that he had heard that I had a beautiful family down here. I introduced Salinas and they shook hands. He told Salinas that she had a remarkable husband and he knew she had her hands full. He looked at me and said he now thought that we had a better understanding of each other and could better work together. As we shook hands, he said that I was cleared to have my C-130s travel in the area off Panama. He said that if we were to inter Columbian air space I should get their approval first. He wished me luck on my war on drugs and said to keep in touch.

The Director walked off and Salinas took my hand and invited me to have breakfast at Angee's. As we walked I told her I loved her and was looking forward to our two weeks together, Salinas said she thought I had forgotten.

I sent for Fernando and set up a meeting on Andros, I wanted the entire group to know our plans. Jerry would come in from Mandeville and Omni Tim from Miami would also be there. We would discuss the Vehicle, TESS, Nicaragua, our war on drugs, Cargo shipments to Iran, the future plans of our new base in Haiti and my two to three month planned stay in General Santos. Salinas, Christina, Maria, Evette and Lourdes would also attend. The girls suggested that I invite Lori but I did not.

The meeting lasted longer than I expected and even with getting two rooms at Lucy's hotel, we had Mike bring over the "Defiance" for more sleeping space. We mapped out a six month plan that we considered included a plan A & B for each scenario. The plan would include Salinas and I revisiting the Haitian General in charge to negotiate the purchase of the Paix airport and the surrounding land to the south, our Andros C-130 making trips to what we called the drug zone, and the design and building of the required sonar for the Vehicle to be able to move it out of its hanger and back from the channel. One of our C-130s would be taken out of service for at least 4 months as G.D. would barrow it installing and testing TESS and a newer smaller GPS guided missile. Jack would go along with this C-130 with its crew, a small security crew and of course his Cindy, his soon to be bride, Cindy. Yes finally Cindy and Jack were going to marry.

Salinas and I would cross back to Nassau on the "Defiance" while Tommy would make a run to Miami, then Mandeville and back to Nassau. I would spend Friday night, with both Salinas and myself stopping in to visit with Malcolm. Malcolm looked beat but said he hadn't missed a day of work and would be ready for tomorrow's trip. Tommy would return me to Miami on Saturday morning. Angee made sure I was taking a good supply of fresh Crawfish and conch for Lori and Ginger to do some cooking for me.

It had been a week since I had seen Lori, the longest separation of our marriage. Lori said for the first time she had gone crazy with jealously.

Lori's swim coach had called and left me a message on my recorder. The coach said that Lori wasn't ready for her meet this week. I received quite a few messages but this was the most important by far. Nilo's message was that he was now ready to start shipping our fruit. Nilo had already shipped a few containers of hanging beef. Matt, Mr. McKee's man had called saying our General Santos construction projects, including the house were ahead of schedule. I then called Christina and told her that she and Maria should leave for General Santos as soon as possible.

I walked into the bathroom and turned on the shower, I heard the bedroom door shut and in she came. Lori said a shower without me just wasn't the same. Lori asked if I had missed her? That was her last question or any conversation for about two hours. From our shower and a short nap, we would get our stuff together and head out to go sailing for the rest of the weekend. Lori took along some of the fresh goodies that Angee had sent her and we would stop at Scotty's in the grove to do some shopping and pass by the Big Daddy's for Robert's pint of Jim Beam.

As Lori handed him that small paper bag, Robert said "I's thanks you Ms. Lori, yes mam you sure knows how to make a poor man happy".

When Lori and I got aboard the Morgan, Lori went below and stored the food that needed ice, when she came up from below deck, she had on one of her new bathing suits. She saw me looking at her and asked "what" you don't like it? The sleek black top of the two piece just covered what it needed to and was without a shoulder strap. Lori smiled and again asked "what" you don't remember this one? I then said yes, it was one that she had modeled from the weeks before. Lori said she saw my eye's when she had it on that day. I said, yes I like it but it looks a bit different now. Lori, still smiling stepped down the ladder and came up with a shirt over the top. She came and kissed me and said it was coming off just as soon as we left the harbor. I patted her on her butt and said to start the engine and take the wheel. I unhooked the mooring and Lori guided us through the other moored boats and on into the channel.

It wasn't the first smiles of the day I had seen but, I could tell that she was feeling much better about our situation. Once the boat was in the channel just out of the harbor I raised the sails and Lori cut the engine. By the time I reached the cockpit Lori had removed the shirt and flecked it down into the cabin. She then changed the direction a bit and reached over and turned lose the jib then reeled it tight. Where we headed Captain, I asked? She pointed to the end of Key Biscayne and said she wanted to anchor off the lighthouse, swim in, and walk on the beach.

Lori asked about Salinas and the children? I said everyone were doing fine. All were now swimming except Jacque of course. Lori said she didn't think she could wait until she finished collage before bearing us a son. I feel left out she said. I'm not so jealous of Salinas, well maybe a little, but the children, Yours, at six and seven, I know you will be wanting to either be with them or at least near-by. You promised that you wouldn't leave me but what will I being doing all that time you spend with your children? Well I said you'll be so busy by then that you won't even miss me I said.

No she said, I want your word that we can start having our children when I'm 18. Lori said she promised to finish high school, then collage while having our children. I even surprised myself with what I said next. "If you want, you can take that "T" out on Monday". I too want our children. If, you would, get pregnant there will be no turning back. The trouble will start when you can't travel any longer, maybe the sixth, seventh or eighth month. Maybe we'll be unlucky and you'll be limited to your travel early on as Salinas was with her first. When you'll have to stay put, then what? I'll still be business building and traveling I said. I hesitated a moment and then said, I won't handle that very well but, if your strong enough and are sure that is what you want, then its ok with me.

Now I said, about your swimming, if you do your best and don't come home with a metal that won't bother me a bit. But if you don't give it you all, then it will follow you all through life. Remember you're the example for your brother and sister, and yes they will be there cheering you on. Lori then asked, I can have our children now? I said yes, whenever you're ready, but don't forget you will get a college education. Lori with one hand still on the wheel came to me with a kiss.

We would be passing through the Key Biscayne channel at about 4:30 p.m. Lori wanted to hear all the plans we spoke about at the big meeting. During the trip to the channel I talked, bringing her up to date. We will be heavy in General Santos, Haiti and yes even Costa Rica, I said. I told her that I believe that Harbor Island or even Nassau could end up our home.

We sailed just around the Key's point avoiding the shallows. We would anchor just a bit north of the Light house. Lori had brought the boat into the wind and I dropped both the main sail and anchor. Lori at the same time had rolled up the jib. As I finished wrapping up the main sail, Lori yelled she'd race me to shore. She dove over from the cockpit and was still under the water when I went over after her. Lori slowed a bit letting me somewhat catch up. My gun pouch might have slowed me up just a bit but not too many people could swim as fast as Lori.

We reached shore and walked toward the lighthouse. The lighthouse had been repaired since my dad had first started bringing my brothers and me here as kids. I reminded Lori of the stories that my Dad had told us about the lighthouse keeper's last stand fighting the Seminoles. Lori said that the way I told the story she could hear it in my voice that I wished

I could have been here to have helped him. The image that stuck in my head all these years of this lighthouse was one of my favorites. Looking at it now, I wished they would have somehow left it as it was the first time I had seen it. From the climb to the top that Rusty and I had made some 24 years ago, he and I both had climbed down with a musket ball or two and at least one arrow head. I told Lori that I felt guilty that I didn't have any Idea where those items were today. Lori knew that if she didn't pull me away I'd be there until dark. She pulled and we walked north on the beach. The beach wasn't empty, but most people were picking up their blankets and some doing their best to get their kids to come out from the water. We could hear one group of kids calling back to their mom, please mom just five more minutes. Lori laughed saying she bet I never wanted to come out. I said if my Dad had called there wouldn't have been anything to do but to get out. I told her that my Dad didn't give any second calls.

Lori and I walked the beach until about an hour before dark, we then returned to the boat and I pulled up the anchor while Lori started the engine and we headed back into the channel moving west into Biscayne Bay. Once in the bay Lori cut off the engine and I dropped anchor. We were just in time to witness a beautiful sunset. We would have a great dinner and hit the sack early. The next morning Lori was up early making coffee and cooking crawfish crepes. Lori was wearing my favorite, just a T shirt.

We sailed the bay for another 3 hours before heading back in to the sailing club. From there it was back home where I found my recorder had several messages. I checked the messages and then the computer.

Lourdes said that we had received a Morse code message that using the CIA manual that Christina had furnished gave GPS coordination's of an airstrip in Columbia. The message said that the air strip would be used tomorrow morning. Nothing more was said. I asked if she was sure that the message was for us or we had intercepted it? Boss, Lourdes said the message mentioned several times something about a traveling cat. I then sent several messages to Jack and Evette. Both messages were top priority.

Lori came into the room and said the shower was getting cold. We wouldn't want that to happen.

Later that night, I had received confirmation from both Jack and Evette.

The next morning, I would stick close to the phone. Jack and his C-130 crew had been flown back to Andros for the early morning mission. Lori was off to school noting there wouldn't be any Doctors appointment today. I got my kiss and she was out the door.

During the day, I received lots of calls and computerized coded messages. By the time I needed to leave for Lori's swim practice I just couldn't go. I called Chubby and asked that he go in my place. By 5:00 p.m. it was all over.

Jack and our C-130 crew had located the small plane that had taken off from the coordinates that we had received. Our C-130 flying on the small plane's starboard side convinced it to change course and land in Limon, Costa Rica. Jack said our 50 Calabria's shooting off several rounds did most of the convincing. As the small plane landed in Limon, my friend Captain Linearis was there to meet the plane. Our C-130 had also landed and just as Linearis had the two Columbians in custody, our C-130 took off again. Tommy had been in Limon earlier dropping off Tim Fernandez from the News. I didn't know Linearis good enough to trust him that he wouldn't turn around and sell the cargo. I did know that Tim would follow the drugs until he was sure they would be destroyed.

Lori arrived just as Jack and I were raping up. I apologized to Lori, her noting that I shouldn't even think about missing her meet in Orlando on Wednesday. Wednesday was Lori's state swim meet. My reply was that I wouldn't miss it for the world. Lori asked what so important that I had miss her practice? I told her that we had stopped a small fortune of drugs from reaching Noriega. Lori said to please be careful. I told her it was a walk in the park.

Wednesday came and Lori rode with her team mates in their bus while I rode alone and Chubby took the family in his station wagon. We were all off to Orlando.

CHAPTER II

THE STATE SWIM MEET

The meet was to start that morning at 11:00 a.m. As we got to our seats I noticed Mrs. Shinner in the stands. Mrs. Shinner had this big hat but I was sure it was her. I went to her and confirmed that it was her. I asked that she not take any photos during the meet and told her that it would be best for Lori not to even see her until the meet was over. Mrs. Shinner said she agreed and said that's why she had on her ridiculous hat.

Lori's first swim was just after 1:00 p.m. Standing on the block she didn't look nervous, but I knew she had to be. Lori was the only sophomore to be competing. So far her team mates had done quite well against the other teams. One girl from a Tampa school had broken a state record in the 100-meter butterfly.

The starting gun sounded and the girls were in the water. Lori was in second position only until the middle of the first lap. It was all Lori from there. At the turn Lori had a good half body lead. Lori didn't look back, not even once. Lori finished first and managed to pull herself out of the water and get to the second-place girl ready to give her a hand up. Lori could hear her brother and sister yelling Lori, Lori, Lori. Chubby, Lilly and myself had also joined in on the yell. We were still yelling when the announcement came, folks we have a new State record to add to the books. Lori had just broken the state record in the 50-meter free style. Lori looked at us with her right arm straight up pumping her fisted right hand. Lori's team mates then smothered her with hugs, yes the coach too.

We weren't over the hurtle yet, Lori had one more race. Lori would swim the last leg of the four in the 200-meter free style. Their senior was the lead off the first leg. We were in the lead by an arm's length at the end of the first, but that lead was gone by the third leg. With the two teams tied at the last turn of the third leg I saw Lori look two blocks down and there stood the girl from Tampa that had broken the state butterfly 100-meter record. Lori looked for me and I gave her my two thumbs up. Lori nodded her head then looked straight forward getting ready. The Tampa team touched the wall first with a small lead. Both girls had a clean dive, but it looked like the Tampa girl had increased their lead. At the turn the Tampa girl had a half body lead on Lori. It was deja vu, Lori turned it on and at the middle of the last lap the girls were neck and neck. Lori poured it on and won by a hand. Yes, they had also taken the 200-meter free style relay. Again but not so quickly this time, Lori pulled herself from the pool to give her rival a hand up. Again we were all yelling, Lori, Lori, Lori. This time Lori came running to us.

The meet wasn't quite over as yet but Lori's team had clinched State Champs. Lori wasn't told at once but she had just broken her own record.

Lori nor I saw it but when Lori had touched the pool's wall at the end of their 200 meter victory, Mrs. Shinner had flung off her hat and started taking photos. Chubby too took lots of photos of Lori and the team. Lori was now wearing three new metals. Mrs. Shinner said that Lori's metal photos would sell lots of clothes. Lori's adrenalin, those metals, her powerful legs, V'd chest and muscular arms and that great smile would be printed in Sunday's sport section and Burdines's advertisement. Yeah I thought, we were going to see a lot of these photos. Lori asked if I could advance her some of her modeling money. She would ride back in the bus with the team, them stopping and Lori offering to treat the team to, you quested it, McDonalds.

Mrs. Shinner made sure the Sports section of the news papers got a good shot of the team and Lori. Thursday's News Sport sections featured Lori's and the team's triumphs.

Lori and her team weren't the only news in Thursday's News, Tim's news had again caught the front page. The Headlines read, "Costa Rica Joins the Regions War on Drugs". The photo showed a small plane with stacks of small packages alongside. Of course, its registered numbers were seen in the photo and the story mentioned that the registered owner of the small plane carrying the drugs was a well know Columbian coffee grower. Lanieras's name, photo nor any other officials were named or photoed in the article.

While reading the news, Lori now ready for class, stopped by for her kiss. She whispered in my ear, just one step closer. I didn't ask, but I though it meant one step closer for her getting pregnant.

Still reading, the phone rang and I was told by Lourdes to get on the computer. Jack was in a situation, looked like Jack had found another drug plane, this time our radar had picked up two helicopters that were escorting the small plane. Jack said that they were taking on fire and that they too had fired back. Before one helicopter had gone down, it had taken out Jack's inside starboard engine, the engine catching fire, and our pilots turning to the north. Jack said that the engines extinguisher had been activated but the engine was still smoldering, it didn't look good. Jack said they had called in a mayday and were 20 minutes from Limon's airport.

Landing at Limon would bring two problems; Limon didn't have any tower personnel and we had no idea if the Limon fire department would reach the airport in time or for that matter, even respond. The computer was silenced and I called Evette to rush to the Limon airport. Evette said she had heard the May Day and was on her way. Ten minutes passed and Evette called via her cell phone, she had just witnessed our C-130 hit the water just off the beach. Yes she confirmed, we had just lost our C-130. Evette's voice trembling, she said she could see that the plane was on fire when it went down. Evette, Evette I called, was the C-130's head up or down when it went in? Evette said up. Call the Coast Guard I said and get an ambulance on the beach.

It was a tuff 30 minutes before Evette called me back. Evette said she could see a life raft coming up to the beach. Evette counted, one, two, three, four, five, yes six survivors she said. That I said would be the entire crew. Jack was the last to walk out of the water pulling the life raft's tow line behind him.

As Jack came out of the water Evette handed him her cell phone. "Sorry Captain we lost the bird" he said. I asked if everyone was alright? Jack said yes and that he had also brought with him a burned out TESS. Jack said he made the decision to ditch the plane. Jack said he figured that there was a chance that the starboard engine fire would continue to spread well after they landed. The damage that had already taken place wouldn't allow the C-130 to take off again. Jack said he thought that I would have rather ditched the plane in the ocean than let it sit there and burn on the runway. I confirmed that he had made the right decision. Jack said that TESS self-destructed and he used the pry-bar to remove it. I started to hear an ambulance coming in the background. The fire truck didn't show. Jack said that Evette's battery was getting low and that he and the crew would wait at the American bar until I could get someone to come and pick them up. He handed the cell back to Evette but the phone went dead. I had already called Lourdes and had Tommy on stand-by. I called Lourdes back and said to get Tommy on the way to Limon.

Jack called from the American bar and said that he was almost sure they had lost any film that TESS had taken. Jack said that they were waiting for us, it was a set up. Its too bad that the other C-130 in Fairbanks hadn't been ready. Jack said next time the other guys wouldn't be so lucky.

I talked and thanked each of the crew and especially thanked the captain that was able to set the C-130 down without it breaking up. The Captain said that he had lowered the ramp, in order to get the plane to sink a bit faster.

It was now only 9:30 a.m. Tommy should be in Limon by not later than 1:30 p.m. I thought about the shape the men would be in by then. I thought about all the activity that was going all around me but then thought about my promise to Lori. I then thought about the loss of the bird, I no longer had contact with the Colonel that could locate me another C-130 especially at the price I had paid for the one we had just lost. I then called Lourdes and got on the computer. I needed two things, I wanted our Fairbanks unit ready and back in the air and I needed another low engine's hours C-130.

Through coded message I notified G.D. that we had lost our number two bird, TESS had self-destructed as designed and that we had TESS's burned out shell. The communication also noted no loss of life on our side and under what circumstances we put the bird down into the ocean. I also mentioned that I was looking for a replacement off our loss to include the most up dated TESS.

G.D. answered back right away saying that our second crew had been up in the air several times with our C-130 up at G.D. testing several new touches and that it could be ready just as soon as we had a double check of our ground security and the cargo was loaded aboard. The cargo they were mentioning was two types of missiles, one type of which there were 6 of and the second type 16 of. The 6 were the larger GPS guided type, now with a longer range of 50 miles, the 16 were a new much smaller type that could be launched out of the tail with the ramp up or down. The smaller missiles were heat seeking and again for both types of missiles to be fired, TESS's laser system would have to be disengaged.

One hour later, G.D. sent a message that they had contacted the Air Force's Reserve General and we now had a possibility of two C-130s that were ready to move once the General had the DOD approval. No price was mentioned but I knew whom I would be dealing with.

It was no time before Lori came home, with no swim practice she would start getting out of school at noon.

Lori said she had received several invitations to different proms but that the senior prom was this Saturday night. I asked you going? She said we're going. Lori said she had purchased two tickets. Lori said that everyone in school knew she was married to a 38-year old man that she was living with. Lori mentioned that Mrs. Shinner had helped her pick out a prom dress. Lori said with a smile, who knows it might be the only senior prom I get to go to. I thought, here goes that baby thing again.

In another two hours, I received notice that Tommy was in the air on the way back from Limon with our six men and Evette. Evette, Lourdes said had sat in the American bar with the crew. Immigration came and stamped the crews passports in and out, Linearis had come by saying that a group was on the way from San Jose to investigate the crash. Lourdes noted that Evette was as drunk as a sailor and said that Evette didn't want to be the only one in Limon to answer all the questions. Lourdes said that Jack had noted that both Richard and Ian were sitting at the bar with our group. This meant that the CIA would soon, if not already hear of our shoot out resulting in the downing of one civilian helicopter and our C-130.

By now Lori had all the story saying that I could have been in that plane and it not turned out as well as it did.

The Director's office called as well as the Admiral's, then Bob then even Liz. The news had traveled fast that we had shot down what was said to be an unarmed aircraft. All that had called, were more concerned with TESS than anything else. All of this attention made it that much more important to get number three in the air from Fairbanks. The number three bird would still have to fly to Mandeville to be unloaded. If we would have had Paix ready I might have stored the missiles there but, at this point, Mandeville was our only option.

Up until now my businesses had well out paced our spending. General Santos, Paix and the next C-130 plus the new missiles would cost well over $25,000,000.00. No one, but Lourdes knew that we had accumulated over $150,000,000.00 in our overseas accounts, this not including the treasure and other assets such as our stocks, including G.D. and the several paten's.

I put a call in for Jerry, he had already heard the news of our loss. Jerry said it would be hard to step up security at Mandeville and not have the locals notice. My old friend the Sheriff included. It wasn't going to be the space; it was the manpower. Jerry reminded me that he was spending most of his time in Lake Charles with the Iran freight. Jerry asked if I was keeping up with the increase of the inbound freight. Jack said we were going to need Paix sooner than expected.

I then called Lourdes and asked her to move up our appointment with the General. The General wouldn't know just how important the Paix purchase is to us, but then again Haiti always needed the money. I had planned to run the Haiti visit into my promised two weeks with Salinas, but this just couldn't wait. I called Salinas and said to be on stand by for the one or two-day trip, this not mentioning my Saturday nights Prom. Salinas knew how important this trip was and said she'd be ready.

Lourdes came back saying that the General would be waiting for us tomorrow afternoon at 2:00 p.m.

I then called Mr. McKee and asked if he had time for me sometime this afternoon. I mentioned that I wanted an architectural and technical engineer to visit Paix on Wednesday and Thursday of this week. Mr. Mckee said if I wanted it for yesterday I should have called yesterday. Mr. McKee mentioned that I already had his best man. Mr. McKee was referring to Matt who was in General Santos still working on our project over there.

We'd be cutting it close but we would all be meeting tomorrow morning at my apartment. Lori was sitting listening to the entire conversations and said that it would be nice if we had some fresh crawfish and conch so that she and her new cooking coach could have some good fixings for tomorrow's meeting. I said consider it done.

The next morning, I met with McKee and two other men, they arrived just as Lori was heading out for school. Lori had cooked up all kind of fritters and had coffee and fritters ready for the visitors. Lori gave me that big kiss and I love you be careful speech.

I got right down to business, I needed for them to design and build a airport and facility in Haiti's Port of Paix. They could see from the map that there was already a small airport there on sight. My idea was a new runway, this allowing any commercial traffic to use the old runway. I needed three large hangers two off the ground warehouses with office space and living quarters for 100 men. One of the architects said, you want and air force and army base combined, I said yes but that here they would need to add water and electric. And yes it all must be Hurricane proof.

When they were leaving they knew that the first warehouse and the perimeter were my priority.

From the meeting, I was off to Nassau to pick up Salinas and on to Haiti. Salinas looked like a princess, Tommy whom just didn't ever comment on anyone coming aboard said that he'd never seen anyone so beautiful. Beautiful she was.

CHAPTER III
MEETING IN HAITI

We arrived on time and the General didn't keep us waiting. The General asked if we noticed any changes since our last visit. Salinas answered the question saying that the people in the streets seemed more at peace. Well the General asked, to what do I owe this kind visit? Again Salinas, jumped right in and said we'd like to buy the Paix airport and a good amount of property along with it. The Captain, Salinas said wants to move into the château and bring several businesses along to include our air cargo. My brief case was open and I handed him a map of Paix which had the property marked in Red that we wanted to buy.

The General took the map and said that this was quite a lot of property. The General then looked at me and said he had heard that my C-130s were armed and that some of my flights were not limited to delivering cargo but fighting the Cubans. I trust I would still have your support he said. I looked at the General and said that we were at his service just as long as it wasn't fighting civilians. Yes Captain, the General said I also heard that you had your hand in the removal of Marcos. It was time for him to go I said. Well at least he'll die on a beautiful Island with lots of money the General said of Marcos. I on the other hand, he said, I want to die of old age, in peace here in Haiti. Of course, he said, with a good retirement fund. Two million Salinas said. The general said five. I said three million paid to the state and two million paid where ever you want it. The General stood and said we had an agreement. I'll have the land deeds by tomorrow he said. I said the new purchase should be added on to the château, the

General agreed. Salinas stood and the General took and kissed her hand and said maybe when the time came he'd retire somewhere near Paix.

The General never mentioned the five or six family's that were homesteaded on the beach property that he had just sold. Salinas and I would give those families the option of staying put or us moving them further up the coast.

Salinas asked if the château was still to be hers once she turned 21. I said the château and all the property we had just purchased. The company will lease the land from you for 99 years. At my death, you and the children will own the company.

From Port-a-Prince we flew to Paix, Lori and I would stay at the Château while Tommy would return for the two men whom would design the new facility. We were surprised that Sharron was at the airport waiting. Seemed after Salinas had three children with me and is taken care of 3 other children, one mine and the other two of Deanna's, Sharron understood that I was here to stay. Salinas seemed happy to see her mother. We were driven to the château and yes the old man with his shotgun was still posted at the front gate. Of course, the old man wasn't the only guard, the Chateau was still being used to house and train our Haitian militia. Here at the Château there were 10 permeate guards and twenty men in training. The men used the barracks while the barns had been converted into living quarters for more than 50 women and children. Two of the Chateau bedrooms had been converted into a school and one a clinic. Sharron would need to sleep with the help in one room while Salinas and I would get what we called the master. The chateau was a full house. I hadn't realized just how crowded it had become. Salinas seeing the place was ready to leave. I assured her that we'd have it back to normal in a year or less. The place was clean and at least the hot water still worked. It was May and the only air was the ceiling fans and the ocean breeze. Salinas and I stood on the balcony and looked out to the beach. It was a great ten days I said. Salinas, said she knew we would be together after that first day. Salinas admitted that she also knew she would become pregnant during that time. At just 18 she now already had three of our own. No more children for a while I said and she agreed. I told Salinas that within the year most if not all the people would be living in small family homes that each soldier would have. There would be schools and a hospital too.

We passed a quite night and the next morning our people arrived and we spent the day mapping and marking. Both men would take soil samples back with them. Neither man worked directly for Mr. McKee so with some convincing I hired them both. Although Lee was still working the Andros contract, Lee would be the top man on this project too. As in Andros we would use mostly Local workers.

As Salinas wasn't to comfortable with the surrounding and said she missed the children, the four of us departed Paix late that same night.

Tommy would drop Salinas and I off at Nassau and then continue on with the men to Miami. The next day Tommy would return for me. Salinas and I were good, I had said I would take her anywhere she wanted to go for our two week vacation which should start in about 10 days. Salinas wanted to again visit Paris and the Riviera. I spent a few hours with the children, Jacques was so big, at only months old he could hold himself up by my thumbs.

I arrived back in Miami on Thursday night. I was happy to be home and with Lori. Lori had purchased her prom dress and like a wedding dress didn't want me to see it until putting it on for the prom. This even when that same dress was one of the dresses that she would be modeling with on Saturday morning with Mrs. Shinner. I was to either buy or rent a tux for Saturday night. All the jackets that I owned were hand tailored to nicely fit in my shoulder holster.

Saturday morning came and I was excluded from the entire modeling show. It worked out just as well as the number three bird had returned to Andros on Thursday and Jack was ready to get some payback. We had missed a few drug flights that had left from that same runway in Columbia landing in Panama. Lourdes had received the information of the flights but we, at that time were not capable to respond. Friday night Lourdes had received just such a message and Jack had requested permission to fly on over in the number three. Saturday morning Evette hopped on a commercial flight back to Limon while Jack and the number three bird were on their way to Mandeville to pick up four of our heat seeking missiles. We had received little trouble for the knock down of the helicopter that was involved in incident where we lost our number two C-130. Jack and the number three would be in the danger zone just when Lori and I would be getting ready for her prom. I had spoken to Jack about being trigger happy and reminded him that our source inside Panama had said that they had seen children exiting one of the drug carrying planes that had arrived in Panama. It shouldn't be hard to control TESS as thus far TESS's firepower was limited to something with a flame, it shouldn't hit at a helicopter or a small plane unless something with a flame was fired at us. To take one of the copters or small planes down without using TESS, Jack would need to use the big gun or one of the new small missiles that G.D. had just made available.

Lori came home a bit late, coming directly from the hairdresser. Lori came in with a big smile looking very proud of herself. Her hair now a bit longer looked great, it wasn't only her hair that she was proud of. Mrs. Shinner had shown her the weekends Burdines adds, this week showing Lori's big win at the State swim Championship. Lori noted that it was the first time she had been photographed wearing her wedding ring. Lori had worn the wedding ring throughout the swim meet. Mrs. Shinner said she didn't want the ring in the photo but Lori had refused to take it off.

Lori had our night all planed out. She wasn't planning to spend much time at the prom, just one dance she said, that's all she wanted.

I was ready first and was sitting at the computer when she called me to assist her in the dressing room. I couldn't believe my eyes. My 16-year old bride looked like a 25-year old knock out! She was wearing a long black pleated dress cut very low at the top. I hadn't seen her ware anything cut so low unless it was a bathing suit. The dress showed almost too much cleavage but I only swallowed and said how beautiful she was. The dress made Lori's waist line look even smaller that it was. I assisted in sipping up the back. Lori had asked about the diamond neckless, I opened the safe and first brought out the copy I had made, I then changed my mind and put it back, and took out the real one. While Lori was still standing in front of the mirror I placed it around her neck. As I did, from the bright lights and mirror the room started to glitter. Lori wore one carat diamond ear rings plus her diamond bracelet. Lori said it might be a good time to get a kiss, this before she put on her paint. Lori said she understood that a wife didn't need permission to put on makeup when going out with her husband. Lori said we were going to Joe's for dinner before stopping at the prom. While still in the bathroom the phone started to ring. I had told Lourdes that she was to call me on my cell after 8:00 p.m. I glanced at my watch and it was 7:50 p.m. I answered and it was Lourdes saying that we had just located what Jack believed was the same small plane that we had from before, this time without an escort. Not thinking of the time, I got on the computer and called for Jack. There was no immediate answer. Before I knew it Lori was behind me tapping me on the shoulder. I looked back, turned off the computer and we were out the door. Walking behind her I would have been happy to have stayed home.

When arriving at Joe's we weren't put on the waiting list, we were seated as we walked in. Every eye in the place was on Lori.

We were seated only for a short time when the phone was brought to our table. It was Lourdes, not using any kind of code she said there had been another incident. I said to call me on my cell and in 30 seconds Lourdes had called and was on the line. Lourdes said that we had contacted the small plane, and directed them to Limon when the small plane's side door opened and fired what looked like a stinger missile. TESS's lasers were at that moment in the ready mode and had fired back so quickly that the laser hit the missile while close enough to the small plane that in the explosion of the missile, it damaged the tail of the small plane. The small plane then crashed into the sea. Lourdes said that our pilot circled back dropping a four-man life raft at the crash site. It was getting dark and within a few minutes, we lost sight of the debris and the life raft. The only may-day that was sent was ours saying no more than a small plane had ditched, us only adding the GPS location. I told Lourdes to contact both the Columbian and Panama authorities and report sighting the crash and its location. Lourdes's last words on the matter were that Jack said we had it all on film.

Lori sat there not saying a word until I cut the call. Are we ok Lori asked? I replied that we were fine.

Lori and I had a great dinner with Lori holding back just a bit with her not having some of that great key lime pie. The prom was at the Fountain Blue Hilton which had been completely remodeled since I had been there last. The Ball room was incredible. As we came in, there was still that line for couple photos. Lori said she wanted one taken. When it came our turn I was surprised that Mrs. Shinner wasn't there with her crew. As we walked in Lori was spotted by her friends from the swim team and we were seated with them, they had saved Lori and I a seat at their table. Once at their table Lori placed her small hand bag on the table and took my hand and led me out on the dance floor. Me, I probably was still doing that same dance that my first girlfriend Kelly had taught me, but Lori must have been practicing as this girl, my wife, could dance. We danced until the band took a break. When the band returned, we danced some more. Lori and I stayed until the band had packed up and was leaving. We danced all night and had a great time.

Once in the car Lori asked for me to drive to the sailing club, we walked to the dock and right to the launch. We blew the air horn and the night guard who had been sleeping came and took us out to the Morgan. I had left my jacket and bowtie in the car. Lori stepped aboard and turned and had me pull that sipper down while standing in the cockpit. I actually thought that Lori thought that we were going to take the boat out for a sail. That wasn't going to happen just yet.

After about two hours I awoke to the engine starting. I reached for Lori but she of course was gone from the bed. I got up and walked to the cockpit to find her behind the wheel, we were on our way out the channel. Lori had on that black silk no strap braw and that skimpy black silk underwear. Where we headed Captain, I asked? We're going to meet my friends at Sunday's on the key she replied. We're going to have breakfast with the girls then all go for a sail. I was now thinking again and attempted to call Lourdes but my cell battery was down and my spare was in the car. I'd have to wait until we got ashore to use a pay phone at Sunday's. As the sun rose over Key Biscayne we could see it was going to be a beautiful day. I asked if that was the dress of the day and Lori said we'd be putting back on the same clothes we came in and that the agreement that the girls had made was that there would be no change of clothes nor bathing suits. She kissed me and said, the guys too. Thinking about it, I'd already seen most of her swimmer friends in a bathing suit and that wasn't much different than underwear. I hadn't worn white underwear in years and what I was wearing even looked like a speedo. I then asked if her non-swimmer friend Margret was coming sailing with us? Lori smiled and said that yes Margret said she wouldn't miss it but that her boyfriend had to work today at 5:00 a.m. Something about delivering newspapers. Lori thought about it and then said just to let her know if I wasn't getting enough attention. We arrived at Sunday's motoring all the way over. Once the boat was tied off at the dock I got a little more attention, then we re-dressed for breakfast. Two sets of Lori friends were there and waiting, we got a big table and Lori sat with her friends while I used the phone.

Lourdes said she had been up most of the night taking calls and working the computer. Most everything was positive; Jack had checked the film and noted that it almost looked like the handheld missile that the small plane had used miss fired causing the damage that had brought down the small plane. Lourdes said that Jack and the C-130 crew were back in the air this morning looking for any survivors. Lourdes said she had sent notification to the Director as I had instructed.

Breakfast was fun, all five of the girls showed up, Margret by herself and Mel as Lori called her showed up with a different date than she had for the prom. I was sure we would later hear that story. The all day sailing trip was a blast. Lori had put four bottles of champagne aboard, I had forgotten how much fun young people had. I thought of my senior prom, at that time June was my state side girl-friend but I had flown Deanna in from Nassau for the prom. I had no idea that June was pregnant at the time as I had one of my best friends, Alex take June as his date.

Lori was much more outgoing with her school friends than I had been at her age, of course I missed a lot of school where I was either out sailing on the "Princess" or was in Nassau diving for treasure and or fishing. Lori and I dropped off her friends back at Sunday's and sailed back to the sailing club where after hooking up the mooring, used the air horn for Robert to pick us up with the launch. Robert was taken by our dress and how good Lori looked in black. Lori of course had taken most of her jewelry off and had it in her hand bag. We stopped up at the bar to say hello to Paul, Paul's wife Penny was sitting in the bar keeping Paul company. It had been year's since I had seen Penny and Lori and Penny had not met before now. I was ready to get going but when Lori heard that Penny had met me when I was a boy of 17, Lori wanted to hear any stories that Penny was willing to share. Penny also wanted to hear how Lori and I had met. Paul and I had heard most of all this before so we talked about our kids. Paul was surprised that Salinas whom which he had met several times had recently given us another child. Paul had an older girl from his first marriage, he and Penny were on their second, with him saying also their last.

On our way home Lori said that Penny said that we had always only been good friends. Lori said that was hard to imagine, with Penny telling her how I taught Penny to smile. Every time Penny would smile I would reward her with a kiss. I just smiled and said that before being kissed Penny just didn't have a lot to smile about. I mentioned to Lori that Penny had been adopted and that both parents were alcoholics. Lori said that she too had sort of been adopted and it couldn't have work out better.

When we got home my red light on the phone was flashing. I had forgotten to connect my cell phones spare battery once in the car. Lori said to un-zip her before I got to talking. She said she'd wait for our shower.

I called Lourdes and got some extraordinary news, the C-130 had located the raft, the raft was set to give off a signal that gave off its GPS location. The C-130 crew had a visual that there was at least one body in the raft. Jack had the C-130 slow to almost stall speed and went out the back ramp. Yes that hot dog jumped out of the bird doing 90 or so MPH. Lourdes said the Bird had come around and Jack had made it to the raft. Jack radioed to drop a larger raft with an equipment box attached and get a navy helicopter out to them. Lourdes said Jack had found a young female, maybe 12 or 13 years old. Jack reported that the girl had at least a broken leg and so far, was unconscious. Jack had transferred her to the larger raft and set up the half-top canopy. Lourdes said a Navy Helicopter was on the way and would most likely take them to Limon. Lourdes would keep me informed.

I went into the room and found Lori sound asleep. I snuggled up next to her and I also fell asleep. A few hours past and the phone had woken me. It was Lourdes, the Navy helicopter had made their pickup of Jack and the girl and had delivered them both to Limon. Evette was back in Limon and was at the hospital with the girl while the C-130 landed spending just enough time to retrieve Jack.

I sent a message to Lourdes to inform the Columbian Government that one of our planes had picked up a survivor from the plane that had crashed into the sea the night before.

Lori had given her cooking instructor the weekend off. I cooked something and woke Lori. While we ate I brought her up to date on the Panama thing saying I was sure we'd hear more tomorrow from Evette and Jack. Lori was concerned that there may have been other children on board the plane that fell into the sea.

Tomorrow I would be leaving for two weeks, Lori knew but I thought she wouldn't cry until tomorrow. She didn't wait. Lori said she'd be here packed, ready to head to General Santos with the family. Yes when I returned, Lori her brother and sister, Chubby and Lilly would be going to General Santos for about three months, at least this was the plan.

The next morning, I left Lori with her chin up saying she'd see me in two weeks. I wasn't taking much clothes as Salinas would have my bag packed. Before I could check, Evette had called direct via her cell, the news wasn't great. The girl had come too during the night, Evette knew this as she was there by her side. Once the girl came too it was apparent that there was going to be more unexpected problems. The girl still had not said a word but was going thru withdraws. The nurse told Evette that even after two days the girl had heroin in her system. Both her legs had several black user lines. Yes the girl was most likely a heroin addict. The Hospital was asking about the parents or guardian. By now both Captain Lanieris and our friend from immigration had visited the hospital. The only story they got told was that we had rescued her at sea. Not a lie but not the entire truth. Both men knowing that we were active in the area knew there was more to the story but Evette had asked their cooperation, in this case, cooperation meant money.

Evette said that the hospital had set the girl's leg and she was in a hard cast. Evette said it was sad but that the girl had bruises on both her wrists, Evette said the girl had apparently been restrained. The hospital told Evette that they were not equipped to handle this case and that she must be sent to San Jose. Evette said that San Jose said they couldn't help without the parents' permission. I said I make some calls and get back to her. I called Salinas and told her about the girl. Salinas called back and hour later and said to bring her there. I would go with Tommy and pick up Jack on Andros and then fly to Limon and pick up the girl.

Evette sent Dookie to the Limon airport to pick us up, Dookie said the Ms. Evette didn't want to leave the girl. I stopped by the police office to speak with Laneris and then we walked over to the immigration office. Both men were willing to help. Both men signed off on a document that they said could get a adolescents' Judge to sign off on. I didn't figure but the Judge went to the hospital with Laneris to see the girl. After seeing the girl and talking to the Doctors, the Judge had paper work drawn up as me being temporary guardian and the responsible party. The Judge made notes in my passport and wanted a weekly progress report on the girl's progress. Neither myself or Jack speaking good Spanish, Evette would come along on the trip.

It was not so tough as I thought it would be moving the girl as she was somewhat sedated for the trip. Evette held her hand for most of the way. Evette had called Lourdes and Lourdes was on her way on a commercial flight to San Jose and would bus down to Limon. We were still fighting a war and we had already been two days without someone manning the radio.

When we arrived in Nassau, Salinas was there to meet us. Most all of the arrangements had been made. The girl would be admitted into the newest wing of the Nassau hospital that we had donated in Cat's name. One of this wings specialties was drug addiction and rehabilitation. The girl looked terrified as we moved her, still she had not said a word. Evette would go to Hill Top House and get some well-deserved rest while Salinas and Janie's mother would take the first turn watching over the girl.

Salinas knew that this was cutting into her two weeks. Salinas had every day of this two weeks planned, first we were to fly to Pairs for three days then the French Rivera as Salinas would say. Salinas wanted to visit places to see the latest fashions and eat at the best French restaurants. Salinas had planned to take the bare minimum of clothes on our trip as she would buy what she needed in Paris. From the Rivera Salinas wanted to stop over in New York on the way back to Harbor Island. We were to spend our last days of the two weeks at the Harbor Island house.

While Salinas and Janie's mother were at the hospital, I went to the Hill Top beach house and spent the rest of the day with the children. Lori had called Lourdes and her mother said that Lourdes had gone fishing. Lori then called the Hill Top house looking to catch me before we left. When Lori told me what Lourdes's mom had said about where Lourdes had gone, I laughed and asked where she could have gotten that from. I let Lori know what was going on, and Lori said she'd like to come to visit Malcolm on the weekend and would also stop in to see the girl at the hospital. We didn't know if Evette would still be in Nassau, for that matter Salinas and I either.

My time with the children was short, Salinas didn't come home so I went to the hospital. I was surprised to see the girl sitting and talking to Evette. The girl had asked for Evette and Salinas had called Evette and while I was on the beach with the children Evette had gone back to the hospital. The girl now had a name. Carolina, as we thought was 13 years old. Carolina was being used to please the men that were moving the drugs and others. Carolina said that she didn't remember the crash but said that there were two men on the plane. The pilot and the man that fired the round tube. Carolina said that her master was the one that had fired the tube. She only remembered hearing the blast and felt the heat coming from the plane's tail. Carolina said the plane was full of cocaine blocks. Carolina said this was her third time traveling to Panama with that same plane. Miguel as she called him kept her high, giving her injections in her legs. Carolina said that Miguel had killed her mother, father and older brother. She said that the family worked on the coffee plantation of Sr. Morales. Sr. Morales she said was the owner of the plantation and let Miguel do as he pleased. Carolina said she had no Idea how she had gotten into the raft.

The Doctors said that Carolina was going to be ok. She'd be hospitalized for about ten more days being slowly detoxed. Carolina had no other physical injuries but her broken leg. She was afraid to return to Columbia, as she was sure that Mr. Morals would have her killed. Now we had another problem, both Columbia's and Panama's Governments knew there had been a survivor from the downed plane, it wouldn't take much for someone looking for her to follow our trail. Security was added to the hospital and I called Big Ted to put in a heads up. The family in Miami already had full time security, Lori had a team of 6 men that worked two men on with four off. Salinas had a full-time man and the house was surrounded by six men on and six men off. I also put a call into June to offer them security for our daughter Kayla. Not too many people knew much about Kyla but there was always that possibility.

My first thought was to eliminate the threat, then I thought that Mr. Morales was only one of several that could be on that threat list. As I thought about it the list got longer. It was hard thinking about all the problems in the world, Deanna's, Wendy Michelle was almost the same age as Carolina with Johnny not far behind. Hell, even Lori was only four years older than Carolina.

Salinas would go home with me to spend the night. Our Nassau Women Center had a counselor that spoke Spanish and she would spend the night at Carolina's bed side. Salinas added to the news that the Doctors had said that Carolina had recently had an abortion. What a terrible life she has had Salinas said, and me, I'm thinking about going off to Paris to spend money and have a grand time. Salinas said she wanted to cancel our trip. She asked if I didn't mind? We'll still have our two weeks together she said. I hugged her with all my strength and told her I was in love with her.

The weekend came and Lori showed up, first seeing Malcom and then both Lori and Malcolm visited Carolina. Evette was on her way back to Limon; once she was there, Lourdes would return to Slidell. Lori was surprised how pretty Carolina was, Carolina was a beautiful, well developed 13-year old.

That Saturday, Lori went out to pull traps with Malcolm. Sunday morning Lori and Malcolm took out the Hunter. Lori only had 3 more days of school before her summer break. Malcolm had informed Lori, then me, that he would again miss the upcoming school year and wanted to travel with Lori and me to General Santos. Lori said that Malcolm thought he, too, could find a beautiful Philippine girl working on the docks. It was funny but I remembered that Nilo had a pretty daughter that should be about that age.

The next week went by fast, Carolina made good steady progress. Salinas and I flew on over to Eleuthera to spend my last two days with her on the Harbor Island beach. Salinas was sad to see me go as she knew that I be gone for at least two months. Although I didn't mix my time with Lori when she was in Nassau, Salinas had spoken to Lori at the hospital. It was time, I left Nassau for Miami.

Before we left for General Santos I got a call from Liz inquiring if the girl had recovered and asked if she could possibly testify in front of Congress? I hadn't told anyone my plans to depart for General Santos but said that the girl we had plucked from the seas didn't seem to know much and would require at least three months of recovery. Liz said that Congress had inquired about TESS and the girl. I knew it was TESS that had their real interest.

CHAPTER IV

LORI'S BIRTHDAY

It was now the first week in June and we were all packed up and ready to head to General Santos. It would be Chubby, Lilly, Samuel, who was now 6, Melody was now 8, and yes, Malcolm would go too, Lori and her cooking teacher, who wasn't doing too much teaching, a large security team, and good older me. Older I say because before we got back I will have reached 38 years old. Where did the time go.

We had decided to send all the luggage via one of the C-130s cargo trips. Matt was still ordering supplies. All of us would be flying on commercial flights to Manila. Lori and I were anxious to see the progress on the Santos house. The flights seemed to take forever, I remembered several times thinking it was a mistake to even come. Lori and I should have hitched a ride with Tommy. Tommy now had that newer leer, about the same size with more range and a special set of landing gear. The new Leer had also spent two months in Fairbanks.

G.D. was quite busy with all the work we were sending them, the Admiral had offered and we purchased two more C-130s. The first went right into action delivering cargo from Lake Charles to Iran. The other was spending time at Fairbanks, first to well, declassify it, this meaning that my friends the CIA had installed all kinds of monitoring devices on it. Fairbanks said they would use the CIA devices but didn't say just how. All I cared about was clearing the CIA garbage out and G.D. installing all of the latest TESS equipment. We knew the C-130 we were using for cargo was infected with the latest electric bugs, but we needed the aircraft so we used it as it was. The CIA was well aware of our Tehran cargo flights.

Tommy would be meeting us in Manila, he would be flying us to General Santos from there. Here in Manila I knew we were only hours before we reached our destination. Our flight into Manila landed at 10:00 p.m. causing us to spend the night. Tommy didn't want to risk landing on General Santos's grass field at night. Besides the bumpy grass there was the possibility of some of the animals that grazed on the field not moving off fast enough and then there was the rain that could crop up at any time.

We all stayed at the same Hotel where Lori and I had stayed twice before. Lori was secretive about it, but the next morning she was up early and said she had to take care of something important. I thought maybe she was buying a last-minute gift for Nilo and his family. There was also the thought that Lori would revisit that first woman Doctor.

We didn't make it out of Manila until 11:00 a.m. and landed on the grass of General Santos by 12:30 p.m. Christina, Maria and Nilo were at the General Santos airport waiting with transportation. Our C-130 was there sitting being unloaded. As I remembered this was one of the first times I had arrived here that it wasn't or didn't rain. We were all loaded up and headed to the house. As we drove up to the gate I didn't see much except that the front of the house had been painted. Once we walked into the house, there Lori and I could see the changes, before there was one stairway in the center of the house. The center stairway was now gone and there were two stairways one on each side of the main room. The children wanted to see the pool, they walked right through the house heading for the back door. Chubby was right behind them. To their surprise the pool was only half full of water and there were men and women still working on the Barbecue and grounds. Matt was not there as Christina said Matt was over at the refrigerated warehouse, completing some last touches. Christina said the house was basically finished except for the pool and the grounds. The pool Christina said should be ready to use by tomorrow. The kids then wanted to see their rooms. Lori had visited the master and came and took my hand to pull me up the stairs to see it. Lori stopped at the door and told me that I should carry her in. Lori then said it would be here that we would start our family. I scooped her up and stepped in, as I did Lori shut the door behind us.

Lori's morning side trip in Manilla was to revisit that same Doctor that I had first taken her to. This time it was to remove the "T" that the good Doctor had put in more than two years ago. Lori said she had told the Doc all that had passed during the last two years. The Doctor told Lori to tell me that she apologized for the way she had treated me back then. The good Doctor had, as I recalled complained that Americans like me were abusing the young girls of the Philippines.

Melody had come knocking on the door and wanted to show Lori her room and all the nice things that were there. Melody's room looked fit for a princess. Samuel had opened his door and found the surprise of his young life. It was Spotty his dog that was left behind two years ago. Nilo and his wife had taken care of the dog to this point. The house had been extended out from the left and rear. There were now two bedrooms that were placed just in front of the large pool. Each new bedroom had its own small kitchen, bathroom and a separate entrance. The main kitchen now bigger and more open had a bar like opening out to the pool. The house, still had a few things to do to it, but it was beautiful. Christina and Maria had both claimed one of the new pool rooms, this too would kind of separate them from the everyday family life.

The children wanted to revisit the fish factory where they at one time lived, but we wouldn't make it there today. From the house, Lori, Nilo, and I would visit the Fruit station. Nilo said we were now shipping 10 containers of bananas per week, having to use some of the older equipment that the fruit company were still leasing. Nilo said we were now using just under half of our Crowlbe's ship slots. We were also shipping one container of hanging beef and two containers of fish. Nilo said that he had been collecting shrimp for almost three weeks but didn't have enough for a load yet. These shrimp were not the prawns that the the fruit company owned and was shipping, but fresh ocean shrimp caught with nets that were dragged behind one or two of the fishing boats that I had provided to the families that assisted me when I had been injured. The idea here was that Nilo would pay out $1.00 per pound when the fishermen delivered fresh shrimp to our processing plant and then we would split up the profits once brought to market. Thus, so far this didn't look like such a lucrative business to the fishermen, as we hadn't sold any shrimp as yet. Lori said she could talk to the fishermen into this type of work as presently the Fruit Company's prawns were only pulled during the daylight hours.

The fruit plant looked normal until we saw the refrigerated part. Unlike the standard practice of cleaning and bagging in the heat, our bananas were brought in right from the farm and cleaned, bagged, and boxed in a pre-cooled area. In general, Bananas needed refrigeration within 24 hours of being cut. Our system would allow only about six hours after being cut before receiving refrigeration. Our hope would be a banana that was fresher and last longer on the open market. I wasn't too happy but understood that the Fruit company loaned us their containers but our bananas that went into their containers were required to be placed in their boxes and they would just add them to their market. We were receiving the space credit from the shipping line. Our buying the 30 slots from the shipping company was now lowering our shipping cost by $13,000 per week, minus the cost of the unused slots.

The freezer part of the plant would receive the shrimp and fish. The beef plant was much smaller and was separated by almost a mile. This added to the cost but would be more suitable for a buyer that came to visit the plant to see and maybe inspect the beef and its process. Both plants still had men working to complete construction.

The Next day Lori, Malcolm, and I would visit the Tuna plant. I had stopped and purchased flowers I would place at the spot where Joe-Anne had lost her life. During the drive, I told Malcolm the story of the army's attack on the plant, posing as rebels. I told him how Joe-Anne had come out of what was our living quarters firing all 6 shots of her revolver killing three attackers and herself being killed. Lori added that Joe-Anne was a police woman sent by the Government to keep an eye on me but ended up falling in love with me.

The plant manager wasn't expecting our visit but knew who I was and let us in for a walk-through. As we walked in I stopped and placed the flowers telling the manager the story. The manager was not from the Philippines and didn't seem to interested in my story. Lori had my hand and squeezed it to keep me settled. As we walked through the factory Lori noted the spot where she, her brother and sister had lived for the several years before she had met me. The factory was busy with few people knowing Lori or myself. If they did they must have been afraid to speak up. No one looked directly at us. I asked the manager how many workers he employed. The manager said he wasn't sure. I looked at him and told him to start looking for a new job. Lori's squeezing my hand didn't stop my talking. We turned and walked to the door. Then I spotted her, I was sure she was no more than a child. Then another and another, there were children working here. I turned to the manager and asked, you have children working here? The manager pointed to the door and asked us to leave. Please leave the manager said. We walked out and I didn't get in the truck, I just started walking to the Port Gate. Once entering the gate, I went right for the Fruit Company's office. I walked in and demanded to see Mr. Partridge . The woman said that Mr. Partridge was no longer working. Mr. Partridge has retired she said. The new manager I asked? We are presently without a manager she said. I then looked into the small office that we once used, and there sat our old IBM 34 computer. I walked in the door and put my hand on the computer, it was warm, for me meaning it was being used. By now Lori was in there next to me and stood between me and the electric plug. Please Jim she said, please don't do this. I was thinking to unplug the computer and roll it out the main front door to go crashing down the stairs. I would have done this if not for Lori stopping me. I stopped and turned to the women who now looked scared of what I might do. I looked at her knowing she was a Filipino and I asked if she knew that there were children working in the tuna factory. The women looked at me and asked, are you going to stop them? I looked back and said yes mam. The woman came from around the desk and said that her husband's name was John Derrick and that he had come here from the states working for me almost two years. John stayed she said but was fired last year for speaking up about the children. They will also fire me for speaking to you. Where is John now I asked? The woman said that John was fortunate enough to get a job on one of the Container ships. This is my wife Lori I said, the woman said her name was Mitta. Mitta I said, I promise to bring him back. And the children she asked? Yes, I said, we will see to it that the children go to school. Mitta said she was happy that we had returned to our home.

I wanted to walk the container yards but Lori said that I had seen enough for one day. Lori said she wanted to walk the fishing docks. We walked down the stairs and I growled at Nilo him noting my dissatisfaction. Nilo just smiled.

We arrived at the fishing docks to find it much the same as the old days. Lori said before we got on the dock that if I heard any whistling that I better not look. She stopped me when I got out of the car and told me that I have, all I could handle. I looked at her and said yes mam. Lori told Malcolm the story that the first time Lori and I saw each other, she had whistled at me.

She then took my hand and we walked, here the people were much different, when the people saw Lori and I they stopped what they were doing to come and say hello and gave Lori their congratulations. Everyone was happy to see Lori. Many asked Lori in Philippine if it was true that she was a millionaire? Lori just smiled. When it all settled down, Lori said that we wanted to help them all make more money. Let's all be associates in the fish and shrimp business she said. Lori said that we would finance all their gear without charging interest. How about a new boat one man asked? If it works only with us, we will finance I said. I then stopped and said that the Fruit Company's prawns were off limits and that whomever is pulling their prawns must continue to do so producing the same or greater amounts of prawns. One older man asked if I was still an owner or associate with the Fruit Company or the Japanese? I said the only partner that I have is Lori. Then that same man said that it was me that brought the Japanese here. Yes I admitted, you are right and it looks to have been a mistake that together we will have to fix. Most of the captains and their boats were out working and would not return until late afternoon. Lori said we would return at that time.

Nilo was with us and it was then that I told him that I wanted someone from our group to people count the ins and outs of the tuna factory noting if they were Filipinos and or children. I wanted to know how many non-nationals verses nationals and how many children worked there.

From the fishing piers, we went to see Jose at his store and small warehouse. I say warehouse because of all the parts I had sent him. Jose was happy to see us, he thanked me for all the parts I had sent including that special coffee pot. I said that I had owed him one. Jose had figured that I knew he was Ninog but now he could be sure I knew. We didn't talk of his business but of the people. I asked how had it come that children worked at the factory, why, I couldn't understand how their parents would send their children to work there. Jose stated that the children that worked there were coming in from farms where their families weren't getting enough to eat. Its better to have your child working than to have them go hungry he said. Jose said that even where I had donated farm lands to some, they too were having difficulties as the Fruit Company required their fruit to a certain quality and without the help of the Fruit Company and their supplies, that they charged for, the farmers fruit would not sell before it rotted. Jose said he was sure I knew that most of the Fruit Company workers that ate at the company's restaurant didn't get another meal that day. It was true, I did know and had complained about it but hadn't done enough to help.

We returned home, Lori asked what I was going to do.

In Nassau, the problem was different, Nassau had the tourist bringing in the money. The money wasn't distributed as it should have been and it was the girls that Michelle had decided to help stay away from the prostitution and drugs. Here the problem looked to be food. I got on the computer and contacted Lourdes. Louisiana was a large producer of rice and beans. I told Lourdes that I wanted the next flight in to be coming with Rice and beans, lots of it. The problem here was where we were going to store the food. Sure there were a few abandoned warehouses but none that one could store food in that the rats wouldn't get to.

I sent word to my old friend Robin, that I needed another 30, 40 foot refrigerated shipping containers and 10, 20 footers. All of this with matching chassis and underslung generators. I also needed at least 10 used refrigerated containers that I wanted to use for storage of Dry food products. These storage containers didn't require the machinery end but needed to be 100% air & water tight. Robin came back with a lease proposal for the cargo units and a purchase price for the used units. Robin communicated that the new leased equipment could be dropped off in General Santos within 15 days on a special vessel and that used equipment put aboard one of his vessels returning empty to General Santos. These Robin said would be sent on the next ships during the next two weeks.

That evening we had a large group for dinner, Brian was just one of the guest and we all got to talk about some of the problems that we both had here on the Island. For Brian, the ships were losing too much time in port, still not going out full and there were too many breakdowns on the voyage. Brian's other problems were personal as he was staying in my old room at the hotel. A single room with a mattress on the floor and a hole in the floor's corner. The hole in the floor was the bathroom with now two buckets of water.

My problems were all personal. Tomorrow I wanted Lori and Christina to visit the school, we were going to get those children out of that factory and back into school. Lori then added, if they had ever seen the inside of a school. I mentioned John Derrick and said that Brian should find a replacement for him and any of my men that use to work for me that were forced to leave the Island looking for work. I was sure that there was more than one. We had rice and beans on the way that needed to be distributed to those who needed it. We would set up a distribution center in town. I told Brian that we had more equipment on the way and that we would be using 100% of our slots and I believed even more.

Brian's company didn't have any part of the Tuna business except they shipped all it's products. I told Brian that my selling agreement had written stipulations that the plant would be worked by Filipinos. I said that my intentions were not to hinder the plant but that my agreement would be kept.

Me telling Brian this, I was sure that he would get the message to his grandfather and he then to the Fruit Company. Less production of any kind here meant less containers moving meaning less revenues for all. I also needed the shipping line to be making money and stay put or we too would be stuck without a way to move our goods. It all had to work for everyone.

At the table I asked Brian when he was going to take Christina off our hands. Brian laughed and said it wouldn't be while he was still working here. Brian meant here on the Island. Christina then spoke up saying that she had told Brian that once married she would still be working with our group. Brian then added that they would have to talk about that. Christina didn't comment.

From the table Christina and Brian walked out on the porch. I figured that Christina would come back in, maybe the both of them might come back in and ask if Brian could move in here with her. While they were out on the porch I mentioned that possibility to Lori, Lori reminded me of what I had promised her where ever we lived our house would be hers alone. Lori said Christina having a connecting apartment was already stretching it and she would prefer we were living here without Christina.

Lori said she was sorry and that she was hoping that Brian would take Christina away with him.

It wasn't five minutes when Christina came back in crying. Lori still sitting with me asked what had happened? Christina said she had told Brian that she was pregnant and Brian had said she was to have an abortion. For now Brian had said, no marriage and no children. Lori got up to comfort Christina and the both of them left for Christina's room. I thought, life's little problems.

Lori came to the side of the bed and woke me me up for our shower. Lori said that this was all my fault, at least that's what Christina had said. Christina said that she had prepared to get pregnant with me, but I had married Lori. Then Brian came into the picture. My fault, I asked? Lori said yes, you set Brian up with that photo of Christina that you gave his grandfather. I asked, and now you're going to throw her out right? Lori said that I was a SOB, she got out of the shower and got in bed. This was our first pout and I wasn't going to have it. I got out of the shower, put on my robe and was heading for the door. Lori jumped from the bed and beat me to it. And just where do you think your headed she asked? Down stairs I said. Oh no, Lori said you're getting right back in that shower. I thought you were finished with your shower I said. Lori said she was starting over. She said that from now on, there would be no more problems in the shower or the bed.

The next day Lori, Maria and Christina went looking for the school house. The girls found that many children from the farms didn't attend school. Most of the ones that did only went through third or fourth grades. The city kids, only about 200, did much better. The school Mother said that only 20% of the children that started school made it through 12th grade. The school mother even knew of city kids that were now working in the Tuna factory. The children she said only made about 30% of what the adults made but did almost as much work. Lori said there were many empty seats. The school Mother complained that she was short teachers and had no English teachers.

Lori, Maria and Christina then visited the fishing docks to talk with the women folk. Me I spent the day with the fruit consolidation and acting like I was checking the fruits quality. Acting because I knew very little about fruit quality.

That evening Nilo brought the information that I asked for. There were 14 children under the age of 15 working at the tuna plant. Filipinos only made up 55% of the factories workers. First we would attempt to contact the families of the children and speak about their needs. Just stopping the children from working and not solving the families problems, if any, just wouldn't do.

I sent a communication to each of the Tuna Plant owners that they were in violation of our sales agreement. I offered to buy back the operation for the same money that they had paid me plus any reasonable improvements they had made. If they didn't want to sell then they should abide by our sale agreement. Should they continue to violate the agreement then they should move out of the facility within 90 days from their receipt of my communication. I then mentioned that they were to immediately stop using child labor.

The next morning Lori was up before sunrise, the pool was now full of water and she was in there doing laps. As I walked out on the pool porch with coffee in hand, I thought it good that Lori was thinking about the swimming year coming up. Maria opened her door then knocked on Christina's. Moments later both girls were diving in to also start laps.

It was almost an hour and three cups of coffee when Christina and Maria gave it up. Christina getting out of the pool and walking over made me think that she had to be no more than two months along as that body, well it didn't look anything but better than I remembered. Both girls were in great shape. Even before Christina could dry off Maria told her to go change for their little run. Lori could have heard that as she pulled herself out and said she would be right down to join them.

I followed Lori up to the room thinking about something else but when I caught up to her she was already almost changed into running clothes. Lori said she was sorry but that Maria wasn't going to wait for her. Lori asked for me to wait for her to take my shower, as she hurried out, she mentioned that she was going to be in top shape having our baby. I hoped that at least Lori would get through the next swimming year before getting pregnant but without the "T", I figured if not already it would only be a matter of time, a very short time before she was with child.

Today was ship day, we'd be filling 15 slots and already Nilo had enough fruit for five more containers. Next week we would be shipping our first container of shrimp. Things went good with the loading but the ship still left a good 8 hours behind schedule. Brian was there and looked exhausted. He said it wasn't fair of Christina to expect so much of him, he said that yes he would like to get married and start a family, but not now. My grandfather, he said wouldn't have approved that he asked Christina to get an abortion. That's not the way I was raised he said. But even when I've had a few days to think about, I'm not ready to be a father. Brian then said he didn't know how I had made it here.

Lori, Christina and Maria would be in charge of getting the children from the tuna factory into school and distributing the food dry goods that were on the way. Lori said that the families that had sent their children to work in the factory were skeptical of her promises of help, even though she had paid out one month's child salary in advance, this that the children could stay home. Skeptical yes but it had mostly worked. Within just a few days all but a few of the children were no longer reporting to work. Not all the children that didn't go to work reported to school. Lori said that I would need to visit where five children that were still working lived.

The next day Nilo and I would do just that. We visited the large grass hut where the five were said to live. Here there was an older woman that didn't want us there. We were suspicious if the woman was even related to the children, this even though the other children that were living with her called her ma. She had taken Lori's money yet still sent the children to work the next day. The old lady said that Lori had owed her the money and more. The old lady said that Lori had been one of her children but that Lori had runaway coming back and stealing the two of the younger ones. The old women said she took in orphans. Presently she had 10 children, five that worked and five that were too young to work. I asked what had happened to Lori's family and how long Lori had lived there. The woman said that Lori had lived here for almost 8 years, her father and mother were killed when a three that they both were cutting on split and fell on them. Lori was no more than a young child when she was brought here. The two that Lori had come back for, they are not related to Lori I asked? No, she said Lori came back and just took them. The old woman said that she figured that they would get hungry and come back but they did not. Lori had been working down at the docks and I guess she figured that she could feed the other two. I found her but couldn't find the children the woman said. I never saw the two young ones again. What about the two children that Lori had taken, were they brother and sister? Oh, yes, the old woman said, they were dropped off here together by a woman that said she just couldn't care for them anymore. The little boy the old woman said was less than a year old when he was dropped off. Lori then 8 or 9 years old at the time did most of the caring for the baby and the two-year old girl. I wasn't surprised when Lori took them, I was sure they would all be back, but I was wrong she said. I looked at Nilo and then the woman. I asked about the other five children that were working and their ages. The woman gave us the information as Nilo wrote it down. The women asked, you're not going to take them from me, are you? No mam I said, but they are not to return to work, they must go to school. I told the woman to hold all five children back from work tomorrow and Lori would come back by tomorrow morning and take the five to fit with school clothes. Lori would also come with food and take inventory and buy whatever we can to assist you with, however the children are not to return to work.

I had sometimes wondered how Lori and the children had come to be alone. I once asked Lori but she said she didn't remember.

From there I needed to go and find Lori, I didn't, couldn't know just how she was feeling right about now. Lori must have know that I would hear the old woman's story. When we found the three of them, Lori when she saw me came running. Lori first said she was so sorry, she wasn't sure the woman would even remember her but she had. Lori said that she had only lied to me three times, The first saying that she was the children's mother, the second that they were her brother and sister and the third saying that she didn't remember where she had come from. By now Lori was in tears asking me to forgive her. I will never tell you another lie she said, never. Still holding her, I assured her that I loved her that there was nothing to forgive. I did say that I would hold her to her promise not to repeat the past. You're not upset with me she asked? Not at all I said. And the children, Samuel and Melody she asked? Do they have to know they aren't my family. Samuel and Melody have Philippine passports that state their last name as the same as yours was before our marriage, they are our family I said. Lori again hugged me. By now Christina came asking what all the hugging was about. I said that everything was just fine. Christina asked if there was room for one more. Lori turned and hugged Christina saying that she too was a part of the family. Christina hugging Lori with Lori's back to me, Christina then gave me a wink of and eye.

Things were going quite well, the C-130 arrived with the food and more supplies, the storage containers arrived and the then the following week the new refrigerated containers, chassis, and generators arrived. Lori, Christina and Maria had gotten all the children into school and seemed that the three musketeers were spending much of their days together. Lori and Christina were now teaching an English class while Maria taught a Spanish class. Lori had organized the fishermen and we were getting more fish and shrimp into the freezer for shipment. Large decals had arrived from the state's side that would be placed on each side of the leased container equipment, marking our brand logo and name.

Matt had just about finished all his projects but I had one more. Matt also had a favor to ask? Matt wanted to marry his Philippine girlfriend. He asked that I be the best man at their wedding and of course assist with the paperwork to get her back to the US. My last project for him was a house for the orphanage.

It seemed that we'd be billing and receiving about $450,000.00 a week, this once the cargo money started coming in. I figured that this was about the amount of work that Nilo could manage. Not that he couldn't do more but with shipping 20 to 30 full containers, the food distribution center, the two clinics, the school, the orphanage, and his growing restaurant, he'd have his hands full. During the last month, Nilo had more to worry about as Malcolm was hanging with his 16-year-old daughter.

We had been here in General Santos now for almost two months, things were going smooth, Brian had moved back to the states, with his Grandfather sending a replacement. John Derick and all the old crew that had chosen to stay when I had sold the shipping company and Tuna Factory were now back working with Nilo. Our people were assisting the Fruit Company with their containers at least, getting their containers aboard with the correct temperatures. No children were working in the Tuna Factory and even some of the children that were working other jobs in town were now going to school. Some of the Japanese that were working at the Tuna Factory had now packed up and gone back to Japan. Lori and I were doing fantastic; we were quite in love. I had kept close contact with Salinas with her anxiously waiting my return.

Carolina was now staying at the Hill Top Beach house with the family. Salinas said Carolina was doing much better learning how to be a kid again. I wasn't sure about having Carolina spending so much time with Deanna's Wendy Michelle, but the Women's Center and Salinas thought it good for the both of them. Security was still tight and we hadn't heard from Liz again.

Tim from the Miami newspaper was still investigating the drug trade, including Mr. Morals the coffee plantation owner. Seemed that Mr. Morals had several ties to Mr. Gonzales but Tim hadn't found any illegal money movement of Mr. Morals as he had with Mr. Gonzales and his Miami Bank. Besides owning the downed plane that was carrying Carolina, Morals appeared clean. Tim had called Lourdes several times during the last 60 days only to have Lourdes tell him that I was out fishing. Tim's stories had all but gone silence since we hadn't made any more surveillance flights, the last being when the plane that Carolina was in went down. Although we didn't bring the plane down on purpose, we had brought it down.

We had sent Jack to G.D. as they had a new computer that they wanted us to try in the Vehicle. G.D. indicated that if the new computer or modem as they called it was successful then we could build the sonar device that would allow the vehicle to re-enter the cave after a trial run in the channel. Jack with the assistance of our three engineers and divers were removing the cave's computer system so that we could work without the requirement of having to do so in the cave. Seemed everyone was concerned that sooner or later something down in the cave, like the oxygen system or even one of the doors could cause problems that hindered our work or getting in or out of the cave's control station. So far we had been lucky.

Our Haiti construction had now been going on for 45 days. This was in the beginning stage and I wanted to get there just as soon as I could. Matt would be heading that way with his new bride to be, this once he finished up here with the orphanage.

Jerry was now making one a week trips to Tehran. G.D. gave notice that the C-130 they had been working was now being flown under testing and should be ready within the week. Jerry would be short an aircraft for only about a week as we had decided to only debug the second aircraft and at this time, only adding the basic TESS to it. Our two C-130s with the upgraded TESS would not be used for the cargo Tehran flights. This for several reasons, TESS was over protective and could cause several problems that certain pilots may not be able to handle. We were still learning how TESS worked. We hadn't counted on TESS's laser system being so fast, that it could have fired at the flame of the missile that the small plane fired at us, causing the missile to destruct so close to the plane that it had knocked the small plane's tail off. TESS's tracking system, at least on the first upgrade would alert most sophisticated fighter aircraft that they were being targeted when only being tracked, this adding the possibility of the fighter pilot to possibly make the first move. G.D.s take on all this was that for the Vehicle, there were no friendlies, or if there was another Vehicle of the same origin TESS possibly would recognize it.

Fernando in Nicaragua indicated that things there were going well with the Contras in complete control of the southeast and them making weekly raids on things like electric and water plants into the main cities, this including Managua. Fernando said that the regular Sandinista army wanted nothing to do with his black devils. Fernando said that he knew of, arms shipments to the Sandinistas had all but stopped. Honduras blocking from the north, him from the south, the ports being minded and Cuban and Soviet aircraft he thought were weary of our stinger missiles plus the TESS rumors. Fernando again added that it wouldn't be long before the Nicaraguans would be at the negotiating table.

Montibelli had also contacted Lourdes sending a message saying that so much fishing wasn't good for one man. He noted a book to have me read, "Old Man of The Sea". I hadn't read it but had seen the movie as a kid. Montibelli noted that although the book was a best seller, it was very boring.

Miami Tim and New Orlean's Jack and Jody were all busier than ever. Omni had expanded again and Jack from the New Orleans Terminal was busy moving the Iran cargo. Terminal Jack as we called him said that I sure knew how to keep someone busy. Jack was also busy having a bunch of children. He said the more the merrier, he now had three and one in the oven.

I mentioned to Lori that I was about ready to return to Miami. Lori said that she wasn't ready for several reasons, her class she was teaching had three more weeks left, she wanted to attend Matt's wedding which was next week and she wasn't pregnant yet. I asked what the difference would be where she got pregnant? Lori said she wanted it to be here in General Santos. Here she said, where it all started. I said that we'd be here until the last day of school and not a day longer.

It wasn't that I wasn't comfortable here, it was Salinas and the children. In my picture, perfect world, Lori and our children would live on Harbor Island. A few hours Donzi ride or 30 minutes as a Seahawk would fly from Nassau. I pictured the "Defiance" and maybe the "Lori" docked at Valentine's on Harbor Island's west side. I could buy a Grand Cessna and use it to fly back and forth to Nassau. The kids would travel back and forth from Nassau to Harbor Island and vice versa. All of them learning to swim, dive, fish, sail and captain any boat. Haiti's Paix would be Salinas's refuge and General Santos Lori's. This in a picture-perfect world, but that wasn't exactly the world I lived in.

Matt would get married to a beautiful young Filipino girl, the girl Lou now had a Philippine passport with an American visa. Lou, Mi, Christina and Lori were the best of friends. Malcolm was acting pretty strange. Lately, Nilo and his wife being worried that Mi might want to leave with Malcolm, and I was thinking about the possibility that Malcolm might wish to stay. Christina was showing now being almost four months. Christina was still swimming and running with Lori and Maria. Some days it looked like the jogger's club with the six of them running together.

Two weeks later the language classes were over and we were packed up and ready to go. I could tell that Lori would have been happy if we all could have stayed.

This time the children didn't need to leave their little dog, we had arranged a visa, this time Matt and Lou would use Lori's and my commercial tickets while Lori and I would fly all the way back with Tommy. Tommy would be taking the group to Manila, Lori and I making a short stopover in Manila to visit her Doctor checking on if she was pregnant or not.

Malcolm had a hard time at the General Santos airport; it took Lou's mother to pull Mi and Malcolm apart.

Christina and Maria were to stay, Maria saying she didn't want to leave Christina being pregnant. Christina said she was thinking of having her child in General Santos. Both Christina and Maria had grown attached to the children of the school and orphanage. I promised to get Fernando here for a visit just as soon as I could.

In Manila, at that same woman Doctor that had scolded me so badly, gave us the news that Lori was indeed pregnant. The Doctor said she couldn't pin point the date but it was only by weeks. We noted the first week of August. The Doctor said that Lori should visit a doctor within the next month and then each month until she gave birth. The now good Doctor congratulated us both and we were off back to the waiting Leer. That I knew of Lori hadn't mentioned to anyone that we were trying to get pregnant. This was going to be a surprise to everyone. We agreed that we'd wait until the next Doctor's visit to announce the good news. To the leer and once aboard Lori didn't let go of my arm until she fell asleep on my shoulder.

We would beat the rest of the group back by almost a day. I had already gone to Nassau when they arrived in Miami. It was agreed that Lori would start school as she wanted to continue to, yes swim. Lori said she thought she would get through Thanksgiving before having to stop swimming. Somehow Lori thought she could finish her 11th grade by the time the baby came, have the baby and return to 12th grade the next year, anyway that was her plan. It sounded to me like a plan, but we'd see how she felt with me spending so much time away.

I was happy to see Salinas and the children. Salinas looked like a million, better than I ever could have imagined. Her exercising every day, swimming and riding her horses did wonders for her, she looked like, well once in the shower I saw that she had become the most beautiful creature on earth. Her hair now long like the first time I had seen her but now, it shined. Her skin was smooth as silk with a waist that I could almost put my hands around. The difference from that 15-year old skinny girl that I had met in the stables of Paix was mostly her chest. When people talked about Bo Derik and her 36 24 36 and being a ten. Salinas was a 36 20 36, a number 15. Yes and she knew it too. She knew just how to please me. Salinas had seen the Lori and Christina photos, Salinas put on the same color and make bathing suit that the girls had on so I would see after her having three children, she looked as good or better than either of them. Salinas was proud of how she looked.

Looked like Carolina was a part of the family but was skid-ish toward me. Wendy Michelle told Carolina that I wouldn't bite or hurt her. Carolina stayed her distance. I figured it wasn't me but any man. Salinas said Carolina had lots to say but not around me. All the children but Jacques were now walking and swimming. We all had a good time at the beach. I spent two days with the family then Salinas and I would take a trip to Paix and then head to Paris. Yes, Salinas would get her Paris trip and the Riviera.

CHAPTER V

THE BEAST

Paix was hot and dry. The old air strip was the only thing left of the airport. The daily flights from Port-a-Prince were now canceled until further notice. I had heard the saying before but not from Salinas, she said the Château didn't have enough room to swing a cat by the tail. We didn't stay the night.

While there, Tommy got a message from Lourdes that Evette had sent a message that one of Fernando's patrols hadn't returned on time and Fernando had gone out looking for them. Lourdes said that the message was clear but that she had spoken to Evette and Evette seemed worried. Evette had told her that just the month before, Managua had reported losing contact with a patrol from the largest Battalion that guarded what they called the southern line. At that time Evette said the radio reported that a Sandinista patrol of 12 men had disappeared and was feared killed or captured by the Black Devils. Managua when mentioning the Black Devils was of course talking about Fernando's men. Evette had noted that Fernando had reported no such encounter.

Salinas and I arrived in Paris, we checked in to a grand hotel and then Salinas shopped for a restaurant. It had to be French and it had to have a special reputation. I thought to fit, it also had to be expensive. I was wrong about the expensive part, it wasn't. The food was good but best of all Salinas was satisfied.

Then there was the shopping, we went to several stores before she purchased anything. I wanted to let her do her thing but I couldn't leave her. The thought of being watched somehow didn't leave me. I couldn't see a tail even though I looked but that feeling was there with me. In her hours of shopping Salinas only purchased one dress, undergarments and a night gown that I didn't see.

Once back at the hotel I called Lourdes, the time difference was 6 hours ahead, Lourdes, sound asleep answered the phone "Yes Sir Boss", she then said there was no word from Evette on Fernando. I wasn't worried yet but I just had that feeling. It was like the feeling that I had that we were being watched. Salinas was ready for our shower, then she put on the night gown that she had purchased. It lasted on no more than 5 seconds. It looked nice but it didn't have my interest. Oh yes I was now 38 years old.

Once I thought Salinas was asleep, without turning on a light, I got my bag and took it and my clothes into the bath room. Shutting the door then turning on the light. I put on some clear plastic gloves then carefully mixed some chemicals into a small hair gel jar. I washed my hands with the gloves still on then dressed, then cleaned the counter and turned out the bathroom light. Without using any lights that could be seen from the street, I went out the main room door into the hallway and used the stairs to walk down to the first floor. Without using the lobby, I exited the hotel from a side door and started looking. I found a man in a car outside the hotel's entrance parked across the street. I sat at a near-by street restaurant and watched the man. Our room was on the third-floor street side. If the man was watching us, he had a good view of our windows. From the restaurant, I called the hotel and rang our room. Salinas answered. I told her to get up and turn on all the lights. Then wait two minutes turn off the bed room lights then walk to the main door, open it, turn off the lights and then shut and lock herself in the room. Salinas was to go back to bed without turning on any lights. Salinas said she understood. I figured that if the man in the car was watching us, then he might just get out of his car while looking up at our room.

Just as I thought, when the lights of our room came on the man in the car got out and stood on the side walk looking up at the room. When it looked like someone was leaving the room, the man crossed the street entering the hotel. As he had walked, I was ready, I walked to the car and put some of my freshly mixed gel on both front door handles. I then went closer to the hotel to see if the man from the car was speaking to someone. I didn't get the chance as the same man was now on his way out of the hotel.

I went left and out came the driver of the car opening the door and getting in and starting the car. I was sure the man didn't see me, I wasn't sure if he was wearing gloves or not. Less than a minute later I got my answer about the gloves, the man in the car slouched over onto the inside of the door. I walked to the car window and took a better look. I wearing gloves, then using a cloth, wiped the door handle then opened the door. I took his passport, cellular and gun. I then sat the man up and shut the door. I walked back to the door from which I had exited the hotel, I re-entered and walked right through the hotel's lobby and through the front door. There was a taxi near the door of which I got in and told the driver to drive. We pulled forward and I had him make a left at the first block then the next left then another then as he passed the hotel's street had him stop. I gave the driver a $100.00 bill and said thanks. I got out and walked back to the hotel finding the passenger's side door open but no second man. I thought him coming from inside of the hotel in a rush to follow me he couldn't of had gloves on. If he opened that passengers side door, he couldn't have gotten far, but which way could he have gone. He could have made it to a taxi, but I walked west. Before I got half way to through the next block, there he was in the street lying between two parked cars. This man was carrying a gun equipped with a silencer. I took his passport and with the silencer walked to a dark area and fired his gun several times hitting the car of the first man on the passenger's side front windshield. I put the gun back into the hand of this man and walked back to the first man's car to the passengers side and wiped the door handle. With the driver's gun, I fired two shots into the air, then threw his gun in the drivers lap and shut the door. I then ran to the east and just around the corner then turned and ran back. As I ran up the doormen from the hotel were on the street. I yelled "what happened?" The door men just raised their hands. I then went to the car's driver door and opened it with the driver falling out into the street. I turned and yelled for them to call the police. Leaving the driver's door open I rushed back into the hotel and went up the stairs just as fast as I could. I opened my room door and turned on the lights only to find Salinas sitting in a chair with my Beretta in her hand. She put the gun down and came a running into my arms. I flushed the gloves but wanted to keep the passports. I knew there was the possibly that the police could come and search my room. I kissed Salinas and told her that I'd was going to secure the passports that I had collected. Tommy was staying in town and I would go to him with the passports. Salinas asked if someone had gotten killed, I smiled and said no but that they would most certainly have bad hangovers. I kissed her once again put my Beretta back in the suitcase turned off the lights closed the door and quickly returned to the staircase. Should anyone come to the door and asked for me Salinas was to tell them that I was nervous and couldn't sleep and went to see the *Eiffel* Tower.

As I exited the side door of the hotel and walked to the main street, I could see the police cars, two at the hotel's front and another just down the street. The police had found the second man. It would be so nice if they would see it as I hoped they would, both men were Columbian Nationals sure to have extensive records that had fired guns on the streets of Paris. I was sure they were either sent by Escobar or Morales.

I arrived at the hotel that Tommy was staying, I handed him the Passports and instructed him to send the passports via FedEx to Jerry. Tommy asked if Salinas was ok and if the Columbians were in the morgue? I assured Tommy that Salinas was good and that Columbians were by now awakening, quite confused by the hand cuffs and the head ache not remembering what had happened to them. I was sure they would be separated not knowing the fate of the other until much later in the day.

When I arrived back at the hotel I again used the side door and the stairs. Salinas again sitting in the chair waiting my return. No one had come a knocking nor called. It was now almost 5:00 a.m. and time for a nap.

Neither of us could sleep, Salinas now only had two dresses to put on, what she had arrived in and the one she had purchase the day before. We dressed with the same clothes and would go out for a nice French breakfast.

Once on the street I placed a call to Lourdes telling her that she should call Big Ted and Jack to inform them of the two Columbians and that I was sure that these men had either been in Nassau or someone from Nassau had called. Tommy had not filed a flight plan when we left from Nassau so it must have been someone's calculation of where Salinas and I were off to from Nassau.

Salinas ate somewhat of a breakfast and with it I got my what the waiter called French Roasted Coffee. Their coffee was almost as good as my Café Bustelo that I was accustom to, Cuban coffee as we would say. I didn't feel better after speaking with Lourdes, we still hadn't heard from Fernando.

Salinas and I would cut our Paris visit short, we would do some shopping and then that night fly to the French Riviera. Salinas had purchased several bathing suits for herself and of course one or two for each child and their two nannies.

We arrived to the beach and checked in to the hotel and went fast to sleep. We were up at noon and Salinas put that bathing suit on, then, I took it off.

We made it down to the beach by about 2:00 p.m., It was as I remembered, crowded with women. Not just any women, women! Salinas was wearing a two piece and said that she didn't like the fact that I was seeing all these beautiful women some of which were missing their tops. I told her, in public she would need to keep the little of a top she had on, on. Your nude beach I said is on Harbor Island. Us not being on the beach 30 minutes, Salinas said she was ready to go home. It wasn't the sun; it was the women staring at me in my almost worn out American flag speedo. Back to the room I asked? Home she said.

Tommy was somewhere out on the beach but about two hours later we were in the leer headed home to Nassau. Salinas said she missed the children; she asked that I stay a day with the kids and then take her to Harbor Island. Salinas, with her head on my shoulder fell asleep, her last words before doing so were that she didn't need anyone on the beach but the two of us.

While in the air the co-pilot opened the door and asked me to step into the cockpit. It was a message from Lourdes, Fernando had returned with bad news, he had found what was left of our missing patrol. All 8 had been killed by something. Fernando had also found what was left of the missing Sandinista patrol, they too were killed by the same thing that had killed our men. Fernando was on his way to Limon where he would wait for Tommy or have Richard fly him to San Jose, where he would catch a flight to where ever I was so that he could give his report in person. Lourdes said that before his exit, Fernando had suspended all ground operations and recalled all his men back to his two southeastern bases. We answered back that Fernando's flight should be commercial and to Miami.

My first thoughts were not as they should be, I should have been thinking of the men we had lost, but I was not. I was thinking that we may have run across what I had told Fernando to always keep a look out for. 17 years ago, there had been rumors from Nicaragua of a Beast that hunted and ate men. I had a drawing of just such a Beast, it was the drawing I had shown the then CIA Director and the Admiral some years back. The Beast that I had hypothesized was what the Beings of the Vehicle had been hiding from. The rumors were that the Beast had a large laser weapon and a small laser it had used to repair its self. The being of the Vehicle had also had both types of lasers so I believed the rumor could have been true.

Tommy would drop a most likely not to happy Salinas off in Nassau and take me back to Miami. Lourdes was notified of my change of plans.

Salinas was still asleep when I returned to my seat. I thought, why Nicaragua? What would bring that thing back there again or for that matter the first time. The thought of some Beast running around with a laser should have bothered me but it didn't. What bothered me was the Beast must have some form of travel vehicle that could be an overmatch for the vehicle that we had. Our Vehicle was in no way ready to do combat with it's enemy. I wouldn't want to test TESS's defense up against the Vehicle, not to mention something that our Vehicle's original owner was hiding from.

Salinas was awakened with our first refueling stop, we spoke of the Fernando news, Salinas was sad of the news of her country men and for their families. She asked what I would do? I told her that we would find and destroy the Beast, but we would not go into this without a plan. In this case, I said, we didn't know the enemy's strength or numbers.

I had almost lost track of what day it was, Lori and the children will have started their first week of school. I thought about my pregnant 17-year old wife starting 11th grade. The long trip back to Nassau would give me lots of time to think, not just about the Beast but my family. It was maybe the first time I had thought about where I was family wise.

We arrived in Nassau, Salinas's people were there to meet her at the airport. I walked her to the car kissed her telling that I loved her and that I'd be back for the Harbor Island trip just as soon as possible. Salinas would have lots to keep her busy here at our Nassau home.

In Miami, I would be meeting with Jerry, Big Ted, Fernando, Omni Tim, Navy Seal Jack and our best Nasa flight engineer.

When I arrived in Miami Lori should have been at school but as things go she was having her first morning of a heavy upset stomach. She said that Lilly said it was morning sickness, something that went along with being in the first few months of Pregnancy.

Lourdes had let Lori knew that I was on the way and Lori was at the apartment waiting. As I got to the apartment Lori was there to pull me into the shower.

Lori had found that while away we had some work done to the jeep, I also had delivered her a new BMW. Lori was happy with her new car but had not taken it to school. The jeep already being heavy was now heavier, this with a new standard 4 speed transmission and a larger 6-cylinder motor. The new motor was still not so powerful but the old motor just wouldn't have lasted with the extra weight of built proof glass and air-conditioning. As it was, the 1951 Willys jeep without these up-grades looked like a tank, now it was a tank.

The apartment soon started to fill up with my guest, Lori was excused to our bed room.

First on the agenda was the loss of our men. All of us except for Big Ted would be Flying to Fairbanks to brief them on what we believed was out there and to receive a few demonstrations including a hand-held Laser that closely matched the one that I had taken from the Cave on Andros. G.D. would also brief us on the upgraded TESS that had been installed into one of our C-130s. Fernando's repot was direct with Fernando showing photos of the bones that were piled. There were bones that the cuts lead Fernando to believe that the only explanation was, some kind of weaponized laser. Fernando thought whatever the weapon, it must have been used from such a distance that the men that had been killed couldn't see what they were shooting at. Fernando said there were thousands of shells spent on the ground without any known results. Fernando said that he had never seen such a stack of bones. The only thing missing were the dead men's heads.

Fernando was adamant that he was going back and find whatever it was that had killed his men, the sooner the better he said.

Second on the agenda were my two friends in Paris. Jerry and Big Ted had lots of news. The two men were closely attached to Columbia's

Mr. Morales. One was Mr. Morales's brother, the other a brother in-Law. Both men were still in police custody. Having been separated since their arrest, neither remembered what had happened to them. Both men had extensive criminal records, being well known to Interpol. The two men were being held on, possession of a fire arm, discharge of a firearm in public, endangerment of the public and public intoxication. Big Ted said that there had already been inquiries into my Paris visit and added that the police just might put two and two together. Ted added that for sure they had been there in Paris for me and for sure the brother would know whom was responsible for them landing in jail.

I looked at Jerry and said to get a one on one meeting with Mr. Morales. Saint Andres Island off the east coast of Costa Rica I said. The perfect spot for a vacation, I added, its owned by Columbia and small enough that we should be able to have some control. Jerry said he'd get on it.

Lourdes had called saying that G.D.would be expecting us this afternoon. Tommy, she added was on the tarmac in Opa Locka. We adjourned the meeting and the men, with the exception of Big Ted, would wait for me in the downstairs lobby.

I went to Lori and said that I be going to Fairbanks and would return late tonight. Lori said she was to see Doctor James this afternoon and Lilly would accompany her.

The men and I traveled to Fairbanks with Tommy, us landing and having a limo waiting. Navy Seal Jack said that he'd prefer we traveled in two taxis. Jack said he was sure that big brother would be somehow aware of our visit and listening.

Fairbanks was ready for us, the first thing I noticed was a change in the security. All of our group had been here before, we were each checked through one by one. This wasn't the first time that I was asked to give up my weapons. Once passing through security we were lead directly to the lab where the show started. First, they had set up a demonstration of two lasers, one firing at the other, this representing a ground held or based laser being fired at the newest TESS armed C-130. The technician said the hand-held laser that I had delivered them has the capability of bringing down any of our aircraft. The G.D. technician asked me to push the button that would fire a laser shot toward a car size model of our C-130. I touched the button and the ground laser was fired and the model fired back with the two lasers meeting only feet before reaching the model. The technician said that the C-130's TESS had intercepted the grounds laser beam before reaching the model. We were all impress, I asked how TESS would do against multiple ground or air missiles or laser beams? The tech answered that the shots coming from the same location, TESS could match shot for shot just as long as the TESS power source lasted. The demonstration was a one on one firing, he was sure that TESS could hold its own against several different locations but wasn't sure just how many. Remember the tech said our power source might not be a match for something equal to or greater than the Vehicle's. The Vehicle he thought could out maneuver and out shoot our TESS. The tech said we weren't sure if the Vehicle could withstand a laser's direct hit, but he was sure that our C-130s would not.

Next, they showed a large rifle like weapon, this is a laser gun the tech said. It can fire as many as three times, each with less power than the first. The fire power is related to the power source. We had sent G.E. one of the Vehicle's power rods but the tech said that it could be years before they had anything that could match size for power. The Vehicle's power rod was 3 inches in diameter and 4 feet long. Handling the Vehicle's power rod wasn't so easily done as it was very heavy and it's interior highly radioactive. The weapon that we were shown weighted about 60 pounds and the tech said most of it was the power source. I inquired how much time they would need to supply us with four such lasers. The tech noted, that if approved, it would take at least a month. Fernando would carry out with him their prototype laser rifle.

We then were taken to a conference room where the next show was a film. I hadn't seen the latest C-130 modification. When the film started, Jerry, proudly pointed out that the C-130 in the film was indeed ours. The tech then pointed out the two attachments, one on the top and one on the bottom of the aircraft. The top attachment was much larger than the bottom, even being smaller I asked about how the bottom attachment would hold up in rough terrain landings. The tech noted that bringing the aircraft in on the water wouldn't do any good for the attachment nor the aircraft. Jack and Jerry chuckled. The tech said that the attachment should stay in tack, as long as both landing gears were down in contact with a hard, semi-smooth surface. The attachments were virtually small satellites. The tech said the high-powered cameras, in day light hours could read the words on a dime that was sitting on the ground. The tech said that they had changed out our old IBM-34 and replaced it with a more powerful G.D. built computer that they had produced using much of the Vehicle's technology. The new computer, the tech said, could keep track and communicate with any existing satellites that passed overhead. This the tech said would overcome the loss of our navigation when TESS was sending its signal to remove the magnetic north. This in itself was a significant accomplishment.

Omni Tim had been up at G.D. and installed our coded communication program. I would have hated to have been required to learn a new code.

The next thing was a video of what the aircraft's screens looked like, first the captain's and copilot's then the Navigators and then the two systems operator's screens. These screens looked like something from a Star Trek movie.

The tech noted a new system that could locate and send a laser beam or shot to a pacific GPS location. The tech said they had also added fuel capacity to add an additional 1,000 miles to the aircraft's range.

The Tech had one more thing, they had designed a defensive ground laser system that was could be TESS guided. Again the video showed how the laser would work from the ground. This system would only work with the newest aircraft that had the satellite like system mounted on the top and bottom. TESS could pick up approaching aircraft and send that information to the ground unit. Here the ground unit would receive the TESS information but the firing of the laser would be controlled by the ground unit. If TESS was out of range then the laser ground unit would work with traditional radar.

I asked how these additions would affect the aircraft's cargo space and speed? The tech's answer was direct; we had lost an additional 30% of our cargo space and 10% of our speed. Jack said it wasn't like we'd have to run from someone. The tech said that the entire systems were rigged as to self-destruct so as not to be removed or stolen. The system could also self-destruct from a coded outside order.

The show was now over, I looked at my watch and knew that I was going to be in hot water at home.

Fernando said he didn't want to wait a month for more lasers and wanted the new C-130 to search the southern zone and destroy the Beast as he noted. I reminded him that the Beast as he called it may just have its own little toys that were better than ours.

I wanted to talk to the G.D. financial people before I left but it was late and they had gone home. I was thinking of the cost of all of this. I called Lourdes and arranged a lift for me to Langley, the rest of our group would fly home. Lori wasn't going to be too happy but I had an idea that just maybe the CIA Director could help with.

Lourdes got a hold of the Director and he agreed to meet with me early the next morning. I called Lori and explained that I should be home before she returned from her tomorrows classes. Lori said she had seen Doctor James that day and he had given her something to help with her stomach. Lori said that Doctor James said she and the baby were fine.

The next morning, I did meet with the Director, he had already heard about the Paris incident and asked what I had planned? I told him I was looking for a face to face with Morals.

I informed the Director of what had happened in the jungle of the southwest of Nicaragua. The Director said they had heard the rumors from the early 70s but had zero proof. It's out there I said, why it's there I'm not sure, but it's there. Again, the Director asked what's the plan? I asked if he could arrange satellite coverage in that area? Not just one satellite, several, enough to search for maybe a crash site of some kind or a camp. You figure this thing could have cashed 15 years ago? No I said it could have been much longer than that, maybe the two beings had fought and our being knocked down the one that we're looking for. The Director looked at me and said that I should have been a science fiction writer. The Director went to step out of the room but before he did, he turned and said there were two confidential files on his desk that I shouldn't touch or look at. And don't leave any of that sticky stuff in my office he said.

The Director was telling me to look at the files, I stood and turned the front page. The files were on Morales and Escobar. I took out my small flashlight like camera and photo'd several pages, I was doing so when the Director came back in. He cleared his throat as he came in and I sat back down. As the Director sat he said that I would get one satellite, one and only one he said. He asked for the GPS location of our men's contact with this, so called Beast and said that within 12 hours they'd be searching for anything in that zone. The Director reminded me that the satellite coverage would be limited to time over the sight.

Now he asked, what have you got for me? What's going on with the Vehicle, those new Star Wars aircraft we sold you, and what the hell are you building down in Haiti?

I told him that we were still learning how to operate the Vehicle, we had sent one of its spare power rods to G.D. The power rod is a rechargeable radioactive battery. Somehow the recharge is performed by an electric turbine that is run by air or water flow when the Vehicle is in motion and a water pump when sitting under water. Whom-ever designed the Vehicle must have come from somewhere that had water or they knew that earth was mostly water. I told the director that we were in the process of building two sonar devices but that we were also testing how the Vehicle could communicate navigationally with existing satellites. I mentioned to the director that the Vehicle's computer thought in Latin. I was sure he already knew but told him again that the Being from the Vehicle must have spoken Latin as all the Vehicles controls and literature were written in Latin. I reminded the Director that our oldest known language was also Latin. You're not saying we're related are you the Director asked? Maybe not I said but these Beings could have been at least visitors for quite some time.

Haiti, I said would be our air base. You mean military base don't you the Director said. He then said that there were several in congress that were worried about my motives. I don't see congress doing enough to fight the war on the drugs that are destroying our children or doing enough to stop the Russians or stopping the use of chemicals weapons on civilians I said. How many of Congress's children are hooked on or using drugs? I bet we'd all be surprised at that number, even the congressmen; and if congress hadn't seen the photos of all those dead women and children with their skin burned off while foaming from their opened mouths then they should. Have you seen those photos I asked? Has the President? I bet not I said, because if he did he would have stopped it. The Director then said that he had stopped it. I knew what he meant but didn't go any further.

I told him that we had debugged the first C-130 and soon if not already he would lose contact with the other. I told him what he already knew, that we had stopped all operations in Panama and were in need of warehousing for our cargo business. Yes, I said we will station the most sophisticated of the C-130s there in Paix and yes they would be protected by our people and TESS. And yes I said, that Haiti had extended our Embassy status.

What's the new C-130 capabilities the Director asked? Well I said, we do have some new radar systems that could be used in predicting weather, that too we will need to do some testing with. Give me your word he said that you won't stir up any trouble without talking to me first the Director said. Well I said, after I meet with Morales I'll let you know something but as far as the Beast goes, I suggest that you pass whatever information you can to us but, I warned him not to attempt to deal with it without us. The Director then asked? Because we are out gunned. Yes sir, I replied.

It was early and Tommy was back waiting for me. I decided to fly back to Fairbanks to talk about money.

I was well received at G.D., they had all the accountability ready. According to them I was a minus $22,000,000. This taking into account of the income that G.D. had from using many of our designs in their other products. G.D. said that the up grading of the other units would be much less as most of the cost had been development. G.E. said that there was an offer on the table for my water pump producing electric design. The offer, $150,000,000.00 was a cash offer from an anonymous source. I figured it was most likely G.D. themselves. I then asked if G.D. had shared in the up-graded TESS system cost and if not since they owned 49% why not. I noted that I should bear 100% of the cost of insulation but not the up-grades. Within the hour that $22,000,000.00 turned into $14,000,000.00 which was still a big chunk of money. I then said that if they were interested in my water pump then I would share 49% with them for $75,000,000.00. I walked out of the G.D. office with them owing me $61,000,000.00.

I returned to the airport thinking about being late again. As it was Lori had gone to school and yes beat me home by 30 minutes. Still I was well received getting a big hug and off to the shower. From the shower to a nap.

Awaking from my nap I asked Lori's house girl about Fernando. The girl said that Fernando had left early this morning with his back pack, and a guitar case, him wearing his fatigues. Then suddenly the feeling in my stomach wasn't a good one. I called Lourdes and she said she hadn't heard from Fernando. Jerry had made it back to Mandeville and Jack was in Nassau. I told her to check with the airlines and Evette and to put Tommy on stand by. Lori was now up and I asked her if she spent any time with Fernando last night. Lori said she only saw him come in. Lourdes called back and said that Fernando had hired a privet jet to Costa Rica and that Evette had not heard from him. I had Lourdes call Evette back and have her check with Richard, either Richard had taken Fernando back into Nicaragua or Fernando was on foot. By now I knew I would be once again leaving Lori. I called Jack in Nassau and brought him up to date asking him to get to Andros and have the newest C-130 ready to fly out with twenty of our best. Jack would have Lee send his Cessna to pick him up for the short ride to Andros. Me I was off for the airport. Lori just reminded me that I wouldn't want anyone else to raise my children especially her's. Lori knew the dangers only to well, as just two years before she herself had rescued me off the waters of General Santos. Lori didn't cry she just said to get home safe.

It wasn't long before Jack, 20 of his Haitians, Dan the only diver we had left besides Jack and myself were on the C-130 and headed for Nicaragua. The aircraft hold had two large canvas covered pieces of equipment. Jack said they had been in the process to move this equipment to our Haiti's location.

During our trip we received two communications, both not good. The first was that Evette had contacted Richard and that was a negative. She had also contacted both of our Nicaraguan bases. The most westerly base said that Fernando had contacted them and 8 of their group were on the way to meet Fernando at a spot just 10 miles east from where we had lost our men. Evette had also reported that she had been trying to contact both Fernando and the group of eight without luck. Jack came to me with a parachute in his hand and said not to worry he be there to push me out. I had never jumped out of a plane before and had said unless the aircraft was on its way down to crash, someone would have to push me. I looked at Jack and said he'd have to stay on board to control the situation. This was the first time I thought about having everything ready for my death. I was about to make my first time ever jump out of an airplane and it was dark out there.

We figured that Fernando might have already made the rendezvous with his men. Knowing what they were after, I was sure they wouldn't be traveling at night. We would parachute at about the sight where Fernando was meeting his men. At a good 50 miles out from Nicaragua's south eastern coast line we had activated TESS. We were now using TESS's newest equipment and had located two container ships and a passing commercial aircraft of who we contacted all three giving them prior notice of a break in the ozone that would most likely cause them to lose there navigation and give then some electrical problems. We estimated that they would be effected for only about 20 minutes as we were moving west at a speed of close to 300 MPH. It wasn't long before the ramp started coming down and we were about to jump. I thought about yelling Geronimo, but it was more like "oh s--t'" stepping off that ramp was the biggest rush I had ever felt. I couldn't see any of the men and as I counted and pulled the cord, I thought I was going to come out out of my suit. Floating down I could see other parachutes but still the ground was black. It wasn't ground that I reached it was tree tops and lots of them as I was dragged to a stop. First I was hanging and then started falling until I was caught up within the many limbs. I slowly cut myself down and when reaching the ground the brush was so thick it felt that my feet hadn't really touched the ground. I found my machete but couldn't cut my way with my machete because there wasn't enough room to swing the darn thing. It was three minutes before I heard a chuckle, it was Jobe, the man that Jack had assigned to watch over me. Jobe was the one man that had been here before, his machete was much thicker and shorter than mine. It was daylight before all 22 of us found each other, it had started to rain and rain hard. The ground quickly turned to mud. Still no word from Fernando or his group. We now were on radio silence using Morse code to communicate. We were moving west at a snails pace. We had two men out front and it wasn't long before we heard the roar of the C-130's engines. The heavy clouds made it impossible to see the C-130 but we knew it was Jack. Jack took one fly over and sent code that Fernando's group were only about a mile in front of us. Fernando finally confirmed that they would stop and wait for us to arrive at their location. The C-130 was up ahead and we were sure it was circling. Jack said that they had located a target but that TESS didn't seemed to be threatened by it. Jack said that the weather would break in about two to three hours, this about the time it would take them to refuel. Jack left as we reached Fernando's group. Jack said we were only four miles from the target, Fernando said where our men had been attacked was at about the same spot. We would move ahead until we found a better spot and bunker down. We moved no more than two miles without finding a spot, not wanting to get too close; we circled our group of 29 and called back our scouts. The 31 of us were now in a small circle virtual lying in the mud. Feet inside, faces facing outward. We did our best to dig in but, as we dug the mud just slid back into the holes. We covered a 360 degree view.

30 minutes hadn't passed when we heard what sounded like a group of helicopters. The rain had slowed and we could make out 4, no maybe 5 soviet copters converging on what we thought was the target sight. Being as far as we were, we would not attempt to stop them. The next thing that happen was, it appeared that all of the copters were under attack. Looked like 3 of the five came apart in the air while the other two, on fire may have made it to the ground. Immediately we started to hear ground fire, the only thing we could see was heavy fast rising black smoke. As the sound of ground fire slowed, some of it seemed to be heading in our general direction. Fernando ordered several men into a tripod and he climbed on top using his binoculars. Fernando jumped down and said that several men were running our way, he thought being chased. He warned the men to keep the watch of the 360 degrees and said not to stand or stop the first group of runners. One, then two men ran right by us without seeing us the third was cut down only twenty yards out to our west north west. Then we saw it, the Beast was at a slow trot still chasing the remaining two men that had passed. Fernando now standing and aiming our only laser weapon, gave the order to fire on the Beast. Fernando fired the laser plus our men on that side emptied their weapons at the moving Beast. The beast still moving forward started to turn our way but was knocked down by our heavy firepower. The beast was knocked from it's feet on to it's back. Fernando was on his way to it. Myself and several of the closest few of the circle were close behind. Fernando jumped on it cutting its head off. Fernando handed me our laser, then with the Beast's head in his left hand, took its weapon with his right ordering all back to the circle. Fernando again yelled to return to the circle and ordered to stay alert. All went silent, we had no idea how many more if any there were. I whispered to Fernando

that sooner or later the Soviets would send another group or the Israelis would appear. Fernando sent out two men to strip the beast and drag it 50 yards to the east, the two men would stay with the body. Only minutes passed and several MiGs appeared, one few over the target site while the others went south and north. Looked like the one was trying to draw fire, but there was none. The rain was slowing and Fernando and I decided to slowly move our group westward. The sight was still smoldering as we approached. I wondered that would happen next, I thought the Soviets most likely had sent in all the copters they had stationed in Managua, but was sure the Sandinistas ground troops and even the Israelis wouldn't be far behind. I still didn't even know what the satellites had shown them. Whatever it is the Soviets also wanted it.

We reached the first downed copter, there were no survivors aboard, the copters's tail looked to have been cut off. We now could hear the roar of what we were sure was our C-130. Jack, now no longer using Morse code said that our TESS was in full mode and the area would soon be filling up with visitors. We still couldn't see the C130 but it was now in the smallest circle it could fly. Jack said they saw no ground movement except for ours. We now split up with Fernando moving toward the center with his group of now 6, with Dan taking one group to circle to the north, Myself, Jobe and the remaining men would circle to the south.

CHAPTER VI

A SECOND VEHICLE

Fernando radioed that he had found what looked to be a crashed Vehicle that was half buried into the ground. Fernando noted that the crash site was old as it was overgrown with brush and vines.

Jack now back and talking said that there were two larger aircraft coming in that could be carrying paratroopers, both escorted by fighters, Jack said that they had picked up their transmissions and all of the aircraft were having navigation problems, Jack suggested he drop one of the two big stationary laser guns that were meant for Paix. I agreed. Fernando's group had in circled the Vehicle and Dan's and my group formed and outer circle. From out of the clouds came two parachutes. One crate was the laser and the other a 400 KW generator. Leaving 10 men on the perimeter with Dan. I headed for the laser and Jobe to the generator. I yelled to Jobe that the 460 volt cable must reach the laser. The lasers base had made a hard landing on small stuff and the laser's weight had flatten it so that the laser was, well almost sitting level. As we ripped off the crating, Jack was making lots of noise. Jack reported that two of the three aircraft coming from Cuba's direction appeared to have collided with one another leaving only a single fighter in the air. Jack said, that fighter had swung off to the north. Then Jack said that the aircraft coming in from the west would be passing within three miles to our south with the possibility of them spotting the smoke of the burning copters. Jack giving us an almost play by play, then said that the aircraft coming from the west were, Israelis and that they had already noted that they had been targeted by TESS, Jack said that the larger aircraft had trouble opening its doors but that several parachutes were now opened and on their way down, I could hear someone in the C-130 counting. I was sure that the Israelis knew who and what we were, but they were determined to still get here. I told Jack to communicate with the Israelis aircraft and let them know that we were on the ground and would would not allow any interference. Another of the C-130 crew was now talking saying that two of the Israelis fighters were coming in honed on the smoke. As the our C-130 crew member said it, the two fighters few by.

As I was ready with the ground laser, Jobe was there with the generator cables. I plugged in the cable to the laser and headed to the generator. Here with the generator we hadn't been so luckily with its landing. The generator was sitting at 45 degree angle. If I hadn't had the experience with the generators in General Santos, I might not have been able to even start the thing. It started and I waited about 30 seconds and flipped up the electric breaker. Jack was back on the radio and said that they now had a green light on the ground laser and it appeared to be ready for use. Jack said that we would be receiving 20 or so Israelis ground troops coming from the south and asked if he should stop them. My reply was to try to stop them with little or no loss of life. I also asked Jack to patch their aircraft into my radio. Jack said I was on and I said who I was and that our radius of protection would not allow penetration. I said we would draw a line for their men not too cross. As I said it Jack guided the ground laser to produce a line that burned the ground. The Israeli aircraft had no way of seeing the beam or the hole that the laser had dug in the ground, but their inbound troops did and stopped short of the burning hole. Jack said that the two fighter aircraft were returning and had armed their missiles. Jack didn't have time to say another word. Unfortunately our ground laser knocked both fighters out of the sky.

The Israelis ground troops held their ground stopping in their tracks. Their were no ejections from the Israeli fighters. Both crews had lost their lives. I then apologized for their loss of life and offered the Israelis GPS coordinates where their ground troops could march and we would pick them up and return them to a neutral location. Jack said that all the remaining aircraft had turned back to a westerly direction. For the moment the fighting was over.

The coordinates were given out but the Israelis troops held their ground. All of this had happen so fast. By the time our satellite had come back around our military had most likely missed it all. Jack noted that he guessed that we wouldn't be refueling with the Israelis again. It wouldn't be long before our Marines arrived. I would send Fernando and two more men to recover and move the beast and it's things including the now two laser weapons to our southeastern base. I didn't want to have anything that our military might want to take off our hands or that might assist in getting them into the Vehicle, a crashed Vehicle that we didn't even know if anything of value was left. Jack had now shut down TESS and the Marines arrived via parachute. A Full bird Colonel was among the Marines and declared he was now in command. His orders were to some how remove the Vehicle, but to do so would need our assistance. The Colonel said they would also need to keep the TESS ground laser under his control. I knew what that meant but was sure he didn't.

They dropped in several large pieces of equipment and dug the Vehicle out, us noting a large section that had been damaged. A large osprey helicopter came in and lifted the vehicle and off it went toward the Costa Rican boarder. The Colonel ordered, then asked that our C-130 escort the Vehicle. I didn't trust the Colonel and we would be quite out numbered so we just disappeared into the jungle. We stopped where the body of the beast had been, Fernando had stopped by and also picked up the Beast's head. The Beast's head had been severed using Fernando's laser rifle. Jack's first laser hit on the Beast almost tore it in half.

I was sure the generator couldn't run very much longer, this because of it being so unleveled. Fuel would have only lasted 3 or 4 hours but I couldn't see it running that long before something gave way. Before we left the Colonel, he had placed a heavy guard on the ground laser.

As we had left and we're at a good distance, we radioed Jack letting him know we were out of range. Jack could and then did activate the trigger that destroyed the ground laser.

We caught up with Fernando and planned to cross the river into Costa Rica, we didn't want to risk the Israelis doubling back to get some revenge. Jobe dropped back to see if we were being followed. Jobe came hightailing it back saying there were two men about 100 yards back. Jobe took two men and moved back, they would set traps to stop or slow the followers. Jobe and is men quickly did what we called the upside down goal post. The U was at the top, opened toward our followers with three points of explosives, one at each of the U's ends and one at the center of the U. The post would be our line that would carry the fire to the explosives. Simple gun powder would be used to connect the explosives. As we caught up with Jobe they were ready, unless the followers could smell the gun power, once they saw the fire line coming at them they would ether run to their left or right. The three blast weren't meant to kill them just to slow them enough for us to get more of a distance from them and again they wouldn't be moving so fast. As Jobe lit the line of gun powder we started out in a trot for the river. We took off and moments later we heard the three expositions.

Once at the river there were small towns on both sides. We commandeered several boats and damaged the others and we were off down the San Jose River moving with the rivers flow. Two of the boats had small motors while mine was the only one that actually started, we tied the other boats behind mine and we were off at a good pace. Our group of Black Devils controlling the southern end of Nicaragua didn't allow the Sandinistas to patrol the river, only the Ticos had patrol boats they called their Coast Guard.

Jack had called in another one of our C-130s to pick up the Israelis but the CIA director changed the order and had one of their C-130s from Panama go and pick them up.

Jack was the one that had sent the message that the generator at the target sight had abruptly stopped throwing a piston. Jack said that our C-130 and the Vehicle had safely reached the Navy base in Panama and that our C-130 would meet back at our Nicaraguan base. Jack messaging would have Tommy at Limon waiting to give me a lift to Washington. Jack's message said to flip a coin, hero or villain, good guy or bad guy.

We had lost the original 8 men and had been fortunate not to have lost more. We hadn't heard any news of the two Marines that had been following us but did know that there had been heavy losses of life by the Soviets and the loss of the 4 Israelis pilots. There was no one but us to tell the story of the Beast and how that went.

For Fernando, he had revenged his men, adding to the high respect that the men already had for him. Fernando wanted to take the Beast's head back with his men but I would carry it to Washington. The Beast's body and all of it's gear would go with Jack and end up in Paxi. Our group now even more on the radar would need the only other ground laser set up at Paix.

72

CHAPTER VII

VISIT TO THE PENTAGON

Me, without a bath, still in fatigues and carrying the Beast's head in a sack, was on my way to Washington to explain what had happened during the last several hours that had caused so much damage and gained our side another what I thought was at least a technical victory. This in keeping the technology in house so to speak.

Of course I called both Lori and even Salinas to let them know I was ok, not just ok but unharmed. Neither understood why I was heading north and not to them. Salinas had invited Lori to Nassau to be there once I did return, both being able to see me at the same time. I still owed Salinas three days at Harbor Island, Salinas offered to make a three some for the trip.

I called Lori back and told her to stay put and that I would see her in Miami on my way to Nassau.

Our trip to Washington was diverted to Langley, Dan had come along as those were Jack's instructions to Dan. We both looked a mess walking out of the airport to our waiting limo. Again we didn't use the limo that Langley had sent, we got our own. The limo driver said he would need to charge extra for the cleaning and de-smell job that he would have to do when we finished with him. If he had only known what was in our sack. The sack was starting to smell.

At Langley we were stripped of our weapons and escorted to a debriefing room. Dan was asked to move to another room an I refused. I was told by the armed guard that it wasn't a request. I then dumped the sack's contents on the floor. This I said, was how our last argument ended.

Whoever was watching us through the window must have decided to step in. Good afternoon the tall older man said. It hasn't been a good day for everyone I told the man. My name is Holt, the man said. We were to meet with the Director I stated. Yes, Holt said he'll be around soon enough. Can you tell me what that is, as Holt pointed to the head on the floor. That there was a murderous animal I said. Then I added, what's left of it. The head on the floor didn't look as it had, besides its head being cut off at the neck, the head also had a few built holes that had caused a mess. How did it happen Holt asked? Well it was busy killing Russians and was caught off guard. How many of you were there Holt asked. That's enough questions I said. I'll wait and speak to the Director. Mr. Holt said that in that case we'd be there a while. Then I said we'll be leaving and we could come back tomorrow. Afraid not Holt said, my orders are to hold you until we have the full story. We are being held against our will I asked? You can go when you tell everything you know Holt said.

I though about it then asked if the Director even knew we were here? Dan and I were seated, as Holt walked by I kicked his feet out from under him and I fell on top of him. The other two men just inside the door lunged forward but as things go, they had run into Dan. By now I was sitting on Holt with his head in a choke hold having him so tight he couldn't move or breath. I said I would be holding him without him breathing until we had our weapons. I wasn't watching Dan, but he had done well and had one man down and had removed the other man's gun. Dan took the gun from the man on the ground and kicked it over to me. As he did I said it had been a long day. By now Holt has passed out from lack of air. I took the gun and said that if they wanted Holt to live they had better get someone in here that knows CPR and clear a way out for us. I then said, he's got about 30 more seconds. The door opened and a woman entered and rushed in and pushed me aside. You jerk she said, you almost killed him. I looked at Dan and asked if she was talking to him or me? I then asked Dan if we should fight our way out or give in to them? Dan said that he knew that he shouldn't have saved any of that treasure money for some future good times. Holt was now breathing, I grabbed him and Dan took the girl. The best I could hope for was a phone call out. It was simple, we walked out holding a gun to each of their heads and there was the phone on the wall. I called out and got Lourdes. Lourdes we are being held in building 54, you got it? Yes sir she said. I hung up, dropped Holt to the floor, handed my gun to the woman as did Dan and we walked back into the room and shut the door behind us.

Once back in our small room, I remembered that I had heard a metal-like thump when I dumped the Beast's head on the floor. Taking a pen that was on the table I bent down to the head and was moving back some of it's hair. Look at this I said to Dan, the damn thing has a large metal section integrated into its scull. As we investigated it looked as if there were some kind of thin cables and wiring that had been melted and cut at the neck from Fernando's laser gun.

Holt now up and tapping on the window asked if I thought that call would save me. I then asked if he'd come back in the room so we could chat again. Dan and I couldn't have heard the phone ring but I was sure it had as the woman came and opened the door and said we were free to go. I looked at her and said my name was Jim and this is Dan. Yes Captain she said I know whom you both are. How about you taking care of my friend down there I asked, it's beginning to smell. The woman said her name was Sargent Heather. Well Heather can you accommodate my friend?

Heather said she would put it in a freezer. The phone rang, Heather picked it up, listened, then said yes mam and handed me the phone. You alright boss Lourdes asked? I said it's been a long day. The Director on the same line asked if we could wait for him until he got there. To be direct sir, we've been here just about as long as we can, it's been a long day and I'm late getting home. We wouldn't want the warden not let me out the next time you want me to come out and play. Ok Captain, Miami or Nassau. Before I could answer him, in walked Liz and Bob and two others. I then asked the Director how long it would take him to get here. The Director said 30 minutes. We'll wait I said but just two things. Holt goes and the girl stays. The Director said, thirty minutes.

Bob; I then said, and Liz; what no food or at least a good cup of coffee? Bob said your looking kind of ruff kid, kind of like the first time I saw you at your Dad's shop. Well, I said, I look better than the other guy. The one that Liz might be interested in is inside on the floor. Liz walked in and came right out. Liz looked at me and asked if we had to have killed it and the 4 Israelis pilots? Bob I asked, no cigar? Then looking at Liz, I asked if she'd heard the recorded tapes? The Israelis were given the order to fire on us I said, so the answer is yes, we were given no other choice. The Beast if it hadn't been so busy cutting down and chasing those Russians might have also taken all of us out.

Heather had walked out with Holt and was coming back in with coffee. Bob said that he was on his way here when Lourdes called. Bob said, Lourdes was worried that you might hurt someone here. This is all your fault I said to Bob; you trapped me into this with a beautiful girl and money. I looked at Heather and said, I was only 15 years old and have been doing this crap ever since. Bob looking at Heather said its always about the girls and she should pay me no attention. I don't know Heather said, they're both kind of cute. Bob told her she needed eye ware.

We made short talk until the Director showed with the Admiral and someone from the state department. First off the Director apologized for the treatment. The Director asked if Heather could take Dan for something to eat. Dan said he follow her anywhere. Heather had now bagged the Beast's head and had sent it off to the freezer.

The Director asked for an update on what had happened since our last talk. The Director of course knew of the loss of my men, and that I was going in to look for Fernando. I filled him in on the rest saying that all the conversations that were picked up by our C-130 were recorded, included the Israelis pilots receiving the order to fire on us. The Admiral asked what had happened to the ground laser and the weapon that the Beast had used. I admitted that we had walked out with the weapon that the Beast was carrying and said that the ground laser must have been affected by the failing generator. The Admiral asked how many other ground lasers we had. I said there was only one and it was being deployed at Paix. The admiral said he wanted all the information on the laser and TESS. I said that the TESS technology was already in their hands and that G.D. was still in the development of the ground laser. The Admiral said he wanted the Beast's weapon returned. I told him the Beast no longer needed it. The Admiral said for me not to get smart with him. I told him that the first weapon was personally hand delivered to the White House and it had disappeared.

The Director noted that the second Vehicle was now on a ship and on its way to Andros. The Director noted that this Vehicle was highly radioactive and had now been covered with a sealed lead based cover. The

Director asked if any of our men had been exposed? I again confirmed that we had not gotten even close to the Vehicle, and that I believed that prior to the Colonel moving the Vehicle the Large hole in the Vehicle had been under the ground, maybe containing the radiation. I noted that the Beast was not radioactive. The Director then asked where I thought the Beast was living? I said that was a good question.

I asked about the Israelis and the Director said he nor the state department had heard a word.

The Soviets on the other hand claimed that a battalion of U.S. marines had attacked them without provocation and were demanding a meeting at the UN. I noticed that Dan was back and I asked if Dan and I could go home and I come back an a couple of days.

Dan and I were soon on our way with Dan saying that he had invited the Sargent to Nassau. Dan said the Sarge like himself was single.

The same limo driver was there and asked about our bag. I noted that it was dirty laundry and it was being washed. Dan was to tired to laugh. In minutes we were back on the leer and headed home. My first call wasn't to the girls, it was to Jack and then Fernando. The Beast's body was to be preserved, not to rot and secured. Jack answered back that after a better look at the Beast's remains, he figured that I'd want another look. It was now after 11:00 p.m. I called Lori and said I should be home in about three hours.

It was great to hold Lori, the hot shower was the best I could remember. I remembered thinking this many times. Lori might have gained a pound or two but I could see no signs of her being pregnant, none. The phone rang many times until I pulled the cord. The house girl answered and took messages. I hadn't been to sleep in a bed for some time.

CHAPTER VIII

THE ATTACK OF PAIX

L ori soon woke me saying that Lourdes was on the phone saying it was important. Lourdes said Jack had sent a message that Paix was under attack. Lourdes attempted to connect me to Jack with no luck. I turned on the computer and there were three messages from Jack. The oldest was good news as Jack said that our last ground laser had been delivered and hooked up in Paix. Omni Tim was who hooked it up but I didn't know if he had left or stayed. The next message was that Paix was under attack. The next message said that the laser had knocked down 4 copters but that ground troops came from the east with several amphibious boats coming ashore from the north. The attack was well planned. Jack said he was on the way back to Andros when the attack started. The attack was made with whomever, planning to steel the ground laser. We lost 27 of our brave solders, plus 10 of our workers and the laser. No they didn't get the laser, it had destroyed itself. Jack noted when our C-130 arrived the fighting was over. Jack and his crew picked up a sub that was heading out to sea toward Venezuela, but Jack returned to see what assistance they could give to the survivors. Whomever attached us, also paid a heavy price. Their's were more than 60 dead and 4 more downed copters, I say more because they were also Russians copters. Most of their dead were Cubans.

The acting captain of our guard had said that once the attackers though the laser had stopped firing, a large osprey came from the north to retrieve the laser. As they discovered that the laser had destroyed itself, the osprey didn't even land. As I was reading, a call from Jack came thru. They had picked up 12 of the wounded and were landing in Nassau. One, a Haitian worker was in critical condition. Jack said Paix was a mess but the attackers had stopped short of attacking the chateau. Jack said that Salinas's mother Sharron, had been a big help and was unharmed.

Jerry was on the way with two doctors, several nurses and medical supplies. I of course got dress and was out the door. I would stop in Nassau and pick up Salinas. Lori wanted to come along but there was just no way I wanted her to see the carnage, wounded, and damages that had been done.

It was day light when we arrived for Salinas. Salinas was dress with what she called work clothes; jeans, boots, and no makeup. She ran from her car into my arms. Still in my arms we turned and went up the steps into the leer and we were off. I had sent several message to several people informing them of what had happen. The only replies were from the Director and the President of Haiti, General Namphy. When Salinas and I landed General Namphy was there on the ground with some of his personal. Jerry arrived at about the same time as we did.

The attack had happened at night when most our our people were just getting to bed. The ground laser hadn't picked up the ground attack nor the small amphibious group coming in. The ground laser was awaken and reacted to the copters of which it quickly took down. Most of the loss of life on the Russia-Cuban side had been in the copters. Our losses were from our front guards on both the North beach side and the east where the largest number had rushed our east side perimeter. It was my first time that I had a heavy guilt, this was my fault for not being prepared. Beside the civilian deaths, and counting the 8 men lost almost two weeks before in Nicaragua we had lost almost 30 percent of our force.

An hour after we had arrived Fernando and Richard were making their landing. Fernando was devastated at the loss of the men including the workers who were mostly locals from the nearby small town. The Haitian President declared three days of National morning. It would take almost that much time to burry them all. Salinas would stay but I, I was back on the leer with Tommy headed to Fairbanks. G.D. already knew I was coming and were prepared for my visit. I wanted two more ground lasers with satellite viewing that would work together from a bunkered control box.

In Nicaragua the laser that burned the hole in the ground to stop the Israelis was controlled by Jack from the C-130. If we would have had that kind of control in Paix and a crew that knew how to use it we could have better survived the attack.

I had also brought along the laser and the Beast's remains. G.D. had already received the news of both incidents where we had lost their two newest ground lasers and that a recovered second Vehicle was now heading to Andros and highly radioactive. G.D's. theory of how the radioactive part happened was that one or more of the power rods had been damaged exposing its radioactivity. The Beast's remains didn't show any signs of the radioactive exposure that the recovered Vehicle would have given it. There had to have been somewhere the Beast called home.

I thought that G.D. might have flinched at the site of the Beast's remains, however, men in white chemical suits put the remains on a cart and rolled it away.

The laser from the beast appeared to be from the same technology from the first laser weapon but crafted for a more rugged use. The other thing was that the power cell seamed to be charged. This part was to me worrisome.

G.D. Said they'd quickly have the two ground lasers replaced but without my required improvements.

It was obvious that the Soviets and maybe even the Israelis would try again for the technology. G.D. had also again upgraded security both inside and out.

There were three items in with the Beast's things that just might help us look for where it had called home. One was what looked like a kind of supper remote control to one of our newest TVs, this not made of plastic but of the hard casing like the laser the Beast had carried. It too had a small battery that G.D noted, was most likely radioactive. G.D. had now been working on this type of batteries for almost two years without getting even close to duplicating it's size verses power. The other two items were two cards that again resembled a metal credit card.

I warned the management of G.D. that they wouldn't have much time before our government would be looking for the body that had been connected to the head. Sooner or later someone up there would notice what I thought had been a more primitive body; modified into almost a machine. I figured that the metal plate in the Beast's head had been an upgraded transplant that could have had the Beast jump centuries ahead.

I returned to Paix and attended most of the many funerals. The Haitian President offered the pick of his crop for replacements for the men we had lost.

Fernando asked to bring back Maria and hire two more trainers, we had lost our top two military personal in the Paix raid.

I spoke to Christina first and she would also be coming back to help with the training. Christina said she had missed me and asked if I had also missed her. Of course I had been quite busy since I had seen her last in General Santos, I said yes but she seemed disappointed in my answer. Christina said she still loved me and looked forward to seeing me in Paix. I imagined that Christina should be about six months or so along with Brian's baby. The girls would leave General Santos on tomorrow's afternoon flight and arrive in Miami on Saturday morning.

Lee would be here with some of his construction crew, the Andros construction project was almost at its end. Lee flew to Port of Prince to recruit as many good men as he could. Janie wasn't to happy about Lee being over here, Lee had told her the smell of death was still strong.

Salinas asked what I would do to the the Soviets? I promised we would chase them from Nicaragua and Cuba. Salinas said that Fernando had told her that I had jumped from the C-130 with the men that had come to look for him. Salinas said that Jobe had told Fernando about his little chuckle of me landing in the trees, watching as I tried cutting myself free. I told Salinas that falling through the air was like being in a good shower with her, hitting those trees in the dark was like taking a cold shower without her. I asked her if she remembered our first cold water shower? Salinas said she remembered, like it was yesterday. We had just come from the beach, she said, I was wearing my first bathing suit. You took me into the shower and then slowly took the suit off. Salinas said that she believed that shower got her holding our first child. Salinas was then proudly smiling while holding me. She then said, I will always be yours and yours alone.

Salinas wasn't ready for our Harbor Island trip, she would stay at Paix until Christina arrived then spend a week with the children in Nassau, then return here. Salinas reminded me that she wasn't pregnant, this because most of the time that we had been together she had been. I'm ready to go anywhere and do anything with you she said, it doesn't have to be Paris or the Riviera, it could be the jungles of Nicaragua.

I would return to Miami today; I planned to spend the weekend with Lori, somewhere just the two of us, where ever she wanted to go. It had been a rough couple of weeks, I didn't need a break but knew that Lori must be feeling somewhat neglected. I went directly from Opa-Locka via taxi to Lori's high school parking lot.

My timing was almost perfect, here she came with a boy carrying her book bag. I was leaning against the jeep when she spotted me. Lori came a running. She jumped into my arms kissing me, leaving the boy standing with her books. The boy looking quite bewildered handed me Lori's book bag and said that he hadn't believed that she was really married. Sorry the boy said, I thought she was just trying to put me off. Lori introduced Bill; Bill this is my husband Captain Jim. Bill then looked at me and asked what branch of the service I was in? Well I said I served in the Air Force but the captain came from being the captain of a fishing boat. Bill said that he'd be happy to keep an eye on Lori. If she needs an escort to the game or the sock hop she can count on me Bill said. See you Monday Lori, nice meeting you captain, Bill said as he walked away. Bill driving or walking I asked? Lori said that she usually dropped Bill off at 25th road. We should have taken him and dropped him off I said. He'll be fine Lori said.

Ok where are we off to I asked? Well Lori said, I could work on my tan, how about sailing down to Key West and having someone pick us up on Sunday night. I asked if she needed to stop at the apartment and she said she had an overnight bag in the jeep. From school Lori and I drove straight to Scotty's in the grove then to Big Daddy's then to the sailing club. I now had a much better cell phone, it charged in the cigarette lighter of which the jeep didn't have one. My phone was about dead but Lori's seemed to be good. I called Lourdes and said I'd be off fishing.

At the sailing club, Robert was there and ready, we got several bags of ice and we also were ready. It was still early for a Friday at the club, Robert would start getting busy after 5:00 p.m.,that's when most people got off work and would start their weekend sail. Robert knew Lori but didn't know that she was now my wife. Wow Robert said, finally going to settle down. Lori said no. Robert said, didn't think so. Lori looked through our gear and pulled out Robert's Jim Beam. Yes mam Robert said, I can always count on the Captain.

Lori and I sailed down to Key West without receiving not one distress call. We arrived at the Key West marina just before dark Saturday evening. Lori as she said she would, had worked on her tan. We showered and would go find some fitters then go bar hopping and some late night dancing. Lori was allowed two non alcohol pina coladas. Lori wore a pair of black sport shorts, her black bathing suit top and white tennis. Me black shorts, a loose Hawaiian short sleeve shirt and my old Adidas tennis. We got back to the boat a 2:00 a.m. We got up in time to catch a taxi and go to see the sun rise. We ate breakfast on the beach and then took in the sights.

Our escorts were already in Key West, I had visually picked them up last night as we left the marina.

We left the Morgan docked at the marina and departed at about 4:00 p.m. via the leer for Miami.

Once at home we were told that Christina and Maria had come and gone. Lori's house girl said that Ms. Christina sure was pregnant. Nether Lori or myself though nothing of the comment.

Jerry had called and when I returned his call, he said he had reached out to Mr. Morales and our meeting was on for this Wednesday on the Colombian Island of San Andrés . Jack said I had mentioned that the Island was just off the coast of Costa Rica when actually it was just off Nicaragua. I told Jerry that I must have missed that day of high school. Jerry didn't think it funny. Jim he said, right in the middle of all three trouble spots. The truth was, until this very moment I was thinking of taking Salinas with me. This to show the son of a bitch I wasn't worried by him. Now having to cover so much from so many different directions. Well I'd take Evette, Evette would be needed any way just in case Morals didn't speak English. It was a done deal, San Andrés it was.

The plan was that we fly in with Tommy while Jack circled around the Island in the C-130. Fernando would be in charge of ground security with Jack in the air.

It was Monday morning and Lori was off to school and me off to Nassau. Christina had sent a message to Lourdes that she needed a privet meeting before she and Maria left Nassau for Paix. I could also get some time in with the children.

My friends from G.D. had sent word that they had a few toys ready for some testing. What they had was 2 of the 4 rifle lasers that they had promised. Tommy and Fernando flew up to Fairbanks to receive the weapons. Who knew maybe they'd come in handy on San Andres.

I had promised Lori to take her to at least this Thursday nights football game, nothing was said about the sock hop afterwards.

I arrived in Nassau via Chalk's Airline, what a mind blast from the past. I wondered if the big Bahamian woman still worked in Miami?

I was surprised who picked me up at the airport. A pleasant surprise, it was Salinas. She said she wanted to get me into a good hot shower before anyone could get my attention. Again I had no idea what she meant but I was certainly good with the shower thing and seeing the children.

The next morning Christina was at the gate, I was already having coffee out on the deck. I invited her in but she said she wanted to walk on the beach. Christina was pregnant, a big belly. I of course knew she was pregnant but, wow how big she was. We hadn't walked far, she stopped and said the baby was ours, not Brian's but ours. Christina asked if I remembered when she told me of her plan to give Salinas a break, and while Salinas took this year off from having babies, she would have a baby for us. Christina said that she had already been to the Doctor. It wasn't long after that Christina said, when I went to General Santos with Lori and got married. Just weeks after that she met Brian. She was off on her dates but after seeing the doctor and having an ultrasound the due date matches the last time we were together. I looked at her and said I was happy but that this would most likely devastate Lori. I did not embrace or kiss her. I wanted to but did not. She also wanted to do the same but, she seemed to understand. I asked whom knew and she said only Maria and Salinas. Christina said that Salinas said she was ok with it and they agreed that they would go back to their plan before my marriage to Lori. I then told Christina that Lori was also pregnant. Christina asked if Lori's baby was planned? I said yes. Christina then congratulated me as Lori's would be my number seven. Christina asked if Salinas knew about Lori's baby? I said that she would only now know. Surprises all around Christina said.

Our walk on the beach lasted almost two hours, me catching Christina up on current affairs. Christina had heard most of it from Salinas who was there with me in Paris or from Fernando who was in Nicaragua. She heard about Paix from Jack who was here visiting with Cindy before leaving for Fairbanks to pick up some spares. I thought, at least there were some secrets.

As Christina and I walked up the stairs to the porch, Salinas was up there waiting with more coffee. I looked at Salinas and said "you knew". Salinas said yes number 6. As I gave Salinas a good morning kiss, I sat down and said 7. Salinas said Lori. I said yes. Planned Salinas asked? I said yes. Salinas being the person she was then said looking at Christina, we're going to have to get that girl over here. Not so fast I said, Lori is to finish school. Both girls at the same time said, no she won't. Salinas said that Lori being pregnant didn't change anything. Salinas said she would now be doing all the traveling with me, while Christina took care of the children. Salinas said that she too would be traveling to San Andrés. Salinas said she knew that Evette was on her way here for the trip but she too would be going. I told her that the trip was complicated. Salinas looked at me and said "tell me about it", then she smiled got up and came and kissed me and said how she loved me. Don't worry about Lori, Salinas said we'll all be just fine.

After the last few weeks, I was a bit concerned about how Lori would take all this but I knew I must tell her just as soon as possible. I thought about her sitting in class today and wondered what she was thinking.

By now all the children were up and running all over. Wendy Michelle and Carolina seemed to be inseparable as they were helping in the Kitchen. This was the only house that was big enough for all the children and it would be running out of room soon. Christina had put on one of Salinas's old one piece bathing suits and was now in the pool with Johnny, Michelle, Kelly, Jimmy and Jacques. Of course the 2 Haitian girls that Salinas had helping her with the children were there in the pool too. Salinas watched me as I looked them over. Salinas then came and took my hand pulling me off to our room. The first thing I thought she was going to say, she didn't. She said that it was ok to show Christina affection in front of her. I told her that my feelings toward Christina had changed. Because of Lori she asked? I said in part but that the feeling just wasn't there as it had been. Maybe it was seeing her with Brian I said. Salinas asked if I was going to have a problem having Christina around? I said no that my plans hadn't changed. If Christina wants to stay and your good with it, Christina would be in charge of the children's security, now one of those being hers. I told Salinas that I had never loved her more than now. Salinas said she didn't want me to be the last to know but that Fernando and Maria would be getting married before he returned to Nicaragua again, that at least is what Maria had told Christina. Salinas told me that Lourdes and Evette had both found a man. Not the same one I hope, I said. Don't be silly, Salinas said.

CHAPTER IX

FACE-TO-FACE WITH MORALES

Late that afternoon all the tomorrow's players were at the house checking and double checking. Salinas, Evette myself and ten men including Dan and Fernando would fly in with Tommy. Jack would be circling with another ten men aboard. The newest TESS would be fully activated. Dan and Fernando besides their regular weapons would be carrying our new weapons, those high powered lasers.

We met Morales at a local restaurant, Morales coming with the agreed 6 well armed men one of which stood closer by Morales than the others. My group consisted of Salinas, Evette, Fernando, Dan, two Haitians and myself.

Morales was an older man of about 50 plus years. He was well dress in a $2,000.00 black business suit. He was tall, a good build and olive skin. He did not bother to introduce his people. I, on the other introduced our entire group. Morales said there was no reason for a translator as he spoke good English. Seemed Morales had been educated in the States.

You asked for this meeting, Morales said, what is it that you wish to talk about? Family I said, I'd like to tell you how important my family is to me. We all have family he said. Yes well I want an agreement that we will keep family out of our disputes. You started this problem and now you want to keep your family out of it, he asked? Well I said whom started it doesn't matter, what matters is that yes, I want and agreement that both our families stay out of our problems. Morales then asked if I had family on the airplane that was circling overhead? I said no. The man standing behind Morales then held up a radio and said that they, whom ever was listening, had the green light. Less than two minutes passed by when Jack radioed Fernando saying that they had knocked down 6 incoming shoulder-launched missiles and were tracking the groups that were responsible for the launching. I looked at Morales and asked if he had family on the ground or in the privet plane that he had come in. At the same time Morales's second man received a message that all of the missiles had miss-functioned or exploded before reaching their intended target. Morales then said, no, no family but that his girlfriend was aboard his plane. I nodded to Fernando and Fernando made the call to respond to the shooters but the aircraft was off limits. Morales and his second looked anxious and the second made another call without receiving a response. I looked at Morales and asked if we had an agreement? Morales then nodded his head yes. I then opened my suit case and put in front of him a folder that held a copy of the final adoption papers of Carolina. I said that Carolina would not testify to her past situation unless it was to defend her new family in some kind of international court. I reiterated that we would continue to monitor the air traffic between Columbia, Panama and the US. The agreement would be void should his family be transporting illegal drugs. Morales then asked about his brother and sisters husband that were sitting in a Paris jail. I told him that I had nothing to do with any of the charges so there was nothing I could do. I asked if they had a good lawyer? Morales then stood and asked if there was anything else? I stood and held out my hand, we agree then. Morales said yes we agree, gave his hand and said no family. While standing, Morales mentioned that he had known Benny from New York and that they in the past had worked together. Benny, like yourself didn't approve of my drug business but that he and Benny had done some asset movement together. I said to myself, money laundering. Morales said that he stayed in touch with Jena. I said that I hadn't seen Jena in quite a while. Morales said that Jena was waiting in his jet that was on the runway. I thought what a SOB, Morales knew I wouldn't touch his plane with Jena inside. Jena probably didn't even know we were here, if she knew she'd have been standing here with us.

We were close enough to Costa Rica where we could drop Evette in Limon. Fernando said he needed a few more days in Nassau and it was possible that we were going to have a wedding on the weekend. After the wedding and a short honeymoon, Maria would be going to Paxi while Fernando would be going back to Nicaragua. Fernando would be returning to the spot where the second Vehicle had crashed. The Beast had to have had somewhere to recharge its laser and I wanted that somewhere.

Before we took off from San Andrés we taxied by what Tommy said was Morales's small Jet. I told Tommy to stop, I got out and started walking toward the plane. There was a guard stationed at the door, as I got closer, the door of Morales's jet opened and, down came Jena running. Running like I had never seen her run. She jumped into my arms with a hug not letting go. I thought it was you she said, every time a see a Leer like yours I wonder if it's you. Still hugging me she asked if I had met with Morales? Jena said she'd like to leave with me, now she said. I told her I was with Salinas and she said she understood. Please take me she said. Morales won't mind. He's getting tired of me by now, and I of him.

By now Morales's guard had called his boss via radio and the guard started walking toward us. He then stopped in his tracks, as I took a quick look behind me toward our Leer, I saw that Fernando and Dan were on their way out to us. Jena then yelled in broken Spanish to tell Morales that she would ride with us. The guard then said back, in Spanish that this would cost him his life and to please return. I wasn't quite sure whether the guard meant now costing his life or when Morales got back. Jena then looked at me, kissed me and said she would return to the jet. I asked if she could leave at her own will. She said she would see me in Miami next week. I said to make it Nassau or she could go to Limon and see Evette whom was also in our Leer. Go to the Park Hotel and they will find Evette for you I said. A plane can take you from there to Nassau. Jena said she'd be fine and that yes, she would be in Limon next week. She kissed me one more time and started walking back to Morales's jet. As she walked she turned and yelled that she still loved me. The three of us stood there until Jena walked up the stairs and their Leer's door closed behind her.

Once back in the Leer Salinas asked if it was Jena and what had happen out there on the tarmac? I confirmed that it was Jena, I wasn't sure what had happened but that I hoped that we'd see her again soon.

Just as soon as we were off the ground, I sent a computer message to Jack. Jack said that they had directly hit three of the 6 shooters, the other three were lucky, as there was no clear shot without the possibility of collateral damage.

The rest of the trip went as planned, we dropped off Evette and then departed for Nassau. Limon wasn't big on refueling so we would need to stop on our way home. Salinas hadn't seen Jamaica so we would stop there, get fuel and while the men ate lunch, Salinas and I would go to the beach. I wanted to stop and see how Bev was doing but I did not. I had heard that her grandmother and uncle had both passed away and that Nancy was back living at home. I wasn't sure if I would see Bev again, that it could start something I couldn't in my wildest dreams finish. No, I wouldn't go there.

It seemed strange that Salinas living on the beach was fine seeing and spending time at another one. On the beach, any beach, it brought back memories of those first 10 days we spent together at Paix.

Heck I wasn't even sure Salinas ever took off her bathing suit unless it was in the shower or the bed. I wasn't sure she even owned a brassiere and panties it was always one of those great looking bathing suits. At the beach she dropped off her clothes and bingo there was her suit. Me, I always wore black underwear that looked like a bathing suit.

We were on the beach for only and hour and then back to the Leer.

Once in the Leer, I handed Salinas Carolina's adoption papers, this now made Salinas and I have seven. The 3 of ours, Jimmy that was mine with Cat, Deanna's 2 that we had already adopted and Carolina.

We made it back to Nassau and I got off the Leer and right back on. I would be going back to Miami, hopefully, to spend some time with Lori, it wasn't going to be easy to break the news about Christina's baby, but I wanted to tell her before the wind blew it to her.

Lori wasn't home when I arrived, the house girl said that Lori was at the pool working out with the team. It was early enough to catch her swimming so I took off for the pool.

It was a great feeling when Lori saw me and got out of the pool and came a running. The coach gave me that same look and same speech that I couldn't just walk in and disrupt her practice. Lori apologized and went back to work in the pool. Then Chubby and the children caught my eye. The kids met me half way with Chubby not far behind. I hadn't seen them, any of them in over a month. Samuel said he had heard that I was away slaying dragons. Yes I said it was a fire breathing dragon. Did you bring at least a tooth, Sam asked? I thought about it and said yes, that I would bring it to him the next day after school. I remembered that I still have that tooth from the giant octopus Lusca. One day I thought, Samuel might just show someone that knew about such things and confirm it indeed was a tooth from a monster. Both children said they missed being in General Santos. Of course I said, no home work or bed time.

Practice was now over and Lori was ready to go. She drove the jeep, me the BMW and Chubby his Blazer.

Once Lori and I were home we were shower bound. Lori being a bit tired an not holding her belly in I got the first hint of her being pregnant. When kissing her belly, Lori asked about Christina and asked if there was anything new. I looked at her and it came right out, Christina had told me the baby was mine. Did you kiss her, Lori asked? No kiss no hug, I said. What did you tell her Lori asked? I told her that I had made a commitment to you that I would not break. What did Christina say to that, Lori asked? Christina, I said, said she understood. What will you do she asked? It's what I won't do I said. I have two wives, I suppose it's like June I said. Lori then held me tight and said she loved me.

Later in bed Lori said she would not stand in my way of having a good relationship with Christina and admitted that when Christina announced that she was pregnant, Lori thought there was that possibility. No matter what, Lori said she was happy to be carrying our child but admitted she would always be worried to somehow lose me. Lori said she was confident that it would not be to Christina or even Salinas but to some adventure or someone like Morales. I told Lori not to worry about me that I was the Traveling Cat. Cats have nine lives I said and I've only used up five or so and I laughed. We went to sleep hugging.

CHAPTER X

NORIEGA AGAIN AT JOE'S STONE CRAB

The next morning was game day. I would be having lunch with Bob, then head on down to Lori's practice then catch a good shower with Lori then take her to the Orange Bowl. Lori's high school football team was doing good this year with a 4 and 0 start.

I was looking forward to seeing Bob, he always had news about what was going on. Bob and I were to meet at Joe's, I was there early and as I walked into the bar, I heard this obnoxious laughing that I had heard before. No not Bob's, it was Noriega sitting in the middle of the restaurant with two men in business suits and one in a Air Force Colonel's uniform. I then looked over towards the bar and only saw one young lady that, in my mind, could be with Noriega. When I say lady I meant girl. She looked all of 16. I then checked the area for what could be Noriega's body guard or guards. I spotted a table for two that the two men were looking right at me. I should have noticed them as I walked in but I hadn't. I would need a seat where I could use my small camera to get some shots and have a clear view of the restaurant. The girl was sitting in the bar section that I chose. When I sat two seats from her on her left, I said hello but the girl didn't even turn her head. I noticed that the girl had markings on both wrists. I then got a look at her legs and there were almost the same type of markings at her ankles. As it happened, Bob had walked in and caught me looking at the girls legs. As Bob walked up, he asked if I didn't have enough trouble? Bob then got a better look at the girl and asked what was up with her. I said that I thought she was here with Noriega. When I said the name Noriega the girl looked at me and spit at down at my shoes. As I jumped back to miss the spit, the two Noriega men stood and one was on the way. The man came and took the girl by the arm and pulled her out the front door. Bob said to leave it, but I couldn't. I walked out, following him and the girl. As I walked out the door the man had just slapped the crap out of the girl's face, then pointed her back in. As she walked by me she looked straight ahead. As the man started my way I stepped in front of him. He stopped and said in perfect English, excuse me. The girl I asked, Noriega's property? The man said yes. A little young I said. The man said it was none of my business and I should butt out. I stepped aside and then saw a city of Miami Beach Cop and Metro Policemen standing just across the street looking our way. I crossed the street and asked if they were on detail? The Metro Policeman said for me to move along. I stepped back across the street and used my cell to call Big Ted. Big Ted said he'd have someone there in three minutes and he be there in ten. I told Ted that if he could show up that would be good, that I be inside Joe's with Bob. Bob was now at a table and noted that the girl was again sitting at the Bar. I told Bob that Big Ted was on the way, that I didn't like it that two policemen saw the man hit the girl and did nothing. Bob again said I should stay out of it.

Bob asked about Carolina and how she was doing. I told Bob that Carolina was doing fine and would not be testifying before any of Liz's committees. Bob said that Liz would be disappointed. Big Ted walked in and sat with us a moment. Ted said that the metro cop outside was off duty. I said both cops witnessed one of Noriega's body guards hit the young girl that was sitting at the bar. I said to Big Ted that she looks underage and had what I believed to be markings of being kept tied up. I also noted that the girl most likely didn't speak english.Ted made a call and within 15 minutes two women showed, one in a police uniform the other in a business suit. After speaking with Ted, the two women then approached the girl and as they did the two men got up and were headed toward the girl, Ted stood up and blocked their way. One of them said in a raised voice, "no dije nada". My Spanish wasn't so good but I knew he said for the girl not to say anything. The loud voice got the attention of both the women and Noriega's table. The two women asked the girl to go out side with them, the girl refused. The two men that were with Noriega had now sat back down. The women asked the girl for some ID. Now the Colonel from Noriega's table was on his way over. The police woman stopped the Colonel a good ten feet before reaching the girl. The Colonel said that the girl was with them. The police woman then said good, and asked the Colonel to step outside for a few questions. Now the girl was put in cuffs, yes cuffs. I questioned Ted and he said just to wait. The woman in the suit then walked the girl out. The police woman asked the Colonel what the girls name was, how old she was, where were her parents and how she got the marks on her wrists and ankles? Bob and I were still sitting when our stone crabs arrived. It was a few minutes when the woman in the suit came and spoke to Ted. Ted came back and said that the girl had not said a word, out of what the police woman said was fear. Ted said that the Colonel had talked himself into some trouble. Ted sat back down at our table and said to let the Colonel come back in and sit with us. The Colonel didn't look worried and when he sat, he said he was on a diplomatic mission and that his group included the President of Panama. Ted asked about the girl? Does someone at that table have the girls passport? Ted said that if they didn't have any papers proving she not underage or here legally without a Chaperone, then she was going to be taken down to juvenile. Ted didn't stop there, he then said that if and explanation for the girl wasn't given then the man that struck her would also be taken for a ride. Ted said he understood that the Colonel had told the police that the girl was with them. Ted said we needed some answers now. The Colonel then said he was going to make a few phone calls and walked back to his table. I asked Ted if he wanted some lunch and he said that dinner was going to be on me.

The Colonel now came walking back and handed Ted his cell phone. Whatever was said on the phone to Ted, Ted didn't like it to much. Ted walked over to the two men's table and dropped the phone in the pitcher of ice water. Ted then asked which man had struck the girl? With no answer Ted walked to the door and came back with the off duty Metro Policeman and two more Metro Police. The off duty Policeman pointed to the man who had struck the girl and the other two cops went and cuffed him and walked him out. Ted then turned to the Colonel and said he would need all the names of the men at the table including the Colonel's. The Colonel came back with the names and Ted said that the girl will be held until her parents came for her. And the man the Colonel asked? You can pick him up after his arraignment and bail is set and made. Ted told the Colonel that he should be a bit choosier about his company.

I asked Ted whom the phone call was from? Ted said he didn't know or care. Ted said he'd keep me informed. I thanked Ted and he asked how the things with Morales had gone? I told him as good as could be expected. Ted said he'd stop by the apartment tonight. I then mention that I'd be taking Lori to the game tonight and how about breakfast at the Brickell Town House at 7:00 a.m. Ted said he'd be there.

Bob and I hadn't got to talk much and I was late for Lori's swim practice. Bob said he didn't get out of bed quite as early as us but said how about brunch Saturday morning at 11:00 a.m. I told Bob I'd confirm tomorrow during the day.

I would go to Lori's practice and later to the game. It was funny, when I played here the stadium looked a lot bigger and it seemed that back then there were more people in the stands. Lori's team squeezed out a win and Lori wanted to pass by the sock hop for one dance. Lori said she wanted her friends to meet me and see that she did really have a husband.

I did as she wished, leaving my shoes at the school's gym door. Lori did more talking than dancing. Seemed all of her friends wanted to meet me. When we did dance I felt awkward looking at all these kids. The kids, mostly the boys for some reason looked younger than we were back then. Lori's security escorts were there and I guessed the kids did't notice them but I certainly did, dressed in suits and standing around in their socks.

Lori and I had a good time. Lori had danced with several of her friends including Bill, the boy that was carrying Lori's books. I got asked more than once if I was Lori's father. As it was, my oldest was now only going on 4, Deanna's, Wendy Michelle was now 15, I thought. When I said 15 to myself it worried me a little, Wendy Michelle was now at at the age that I met Deanna and even Lori. Where had the time gone.

That night when Lori and I got home I called Salinas and asked how old Wendy Michelle was? Salinas laughed as she said 15. And Carolina I asked? Salinas said Carolina was 14. Salinas said the next time I was there I needed to speak to Malcolm. Why I asked? Malcolm has been spending more and more time with the girls Salinas said. Salinas said that Malcolm was a hard working, good looking young man. Salinas said almost as good looking as I was. I was quick to ask, what do you mean was? Well Salinas said, the last time I saw you, you was, then laughed. Salinas then asked if I had seen the newest numbers. I asked what numbers, Salinas said the profit numbers. I said no, she said to look. I asked if they were bad? She said to look. Then I heard Christina in the back ground saying to tell him to look at General Santos. I told Salinas that I could hear Christina. Both girls laughed. Salinas asked when I was coming back as I owed her a trip and said to bring Lori with me. Lori was right by the phone and had heard just about everything.

It was late but I called Lourdes anyway. Lourdes answered and I asked for her to send me all the latest numbers from the 6 profit centers. Lourdes said it would only take her a minute. She then asked if I had received the Wedding invitation? Your getting married I said loudly? No sir not me, Fernando and Maria. Damn I said I almost had forgot. I thanked her and with Lori's nudging, I apologized for the late night call. When I hung up Lori asked if I had been told that Lourdes and Evette both had steady boy friends. I said that I had heard something, why? Lori said that she heard that Lourdes was thinking of getting married again. I asked where she heard that from and Lori said from Lourdes. I asked how often she spoke to Lourdes and She said almost everyday when I wasn't with her.

The numbers came in and Lori and I looked together, Nassau sales were reaching right at $250,000.00 per month. I remembered everyone told me we couldn't bring in 2,000 crawfish in a week. With tourist including the shops and boat trips, Nassau's profits would top $2,000,000.00 a year. Then there was the construction business. This year would be off only hitting a profit of about $1,000,000.00 this due to us having to rebuild Paix after it being attacked. Then there was Jacks Terminal, I hadn't spoken to Jack in I believed 6 months, its profits were on the move at just over $3,000.000.00. The Air Transport was also a big winner, but here is where all our extra activity was expensed out. Here we were profitable, but only by about $500.000.00. Our investment portfolio was the kicker. Looked like we were on the way for a record year of profits of over $9,000,000.00, this not including the monies of selling 49 percent of the electric water pump generator. I looked for General Santos and it was missing, then Lori said that it was separated in a different file. It had only been about 8 weeks since we left General Santos but it looked like things had changed quite a bit. Looking at the numbers Nilo must be moving close to 15 banana loads, 2 pineapple loads, 2 beef loads and I didn't know how but maybe 2 shrimp loads and a fish load. This was 22 loads a week that had brought in the week before an estimated $500,000.00 in revenues. At this rate, General Santos could add another $2,000,000.00 in yearly profits to the group. Lori there looking with me said that Christina and her had worked with the fisherman and some of the fruit growers. Lori had ask if we could go partners on two new shrimp boats and maybe start a banana coop with some of the poorer farmers. Lori said that there was another 1,000 hectors to our northeast on the north side of the river that she'd like to purchase. Lori said that the land could be purchased for almost nothing, the cost she said would be the land clearing. You figured all this with Christina I asked? No she said we had help from Nilo. I told Lori it would take more than a year to get out the first container of fruit. Yes, Lori said that Nilo said that it would take almost two years to be in full production.

It was getting late, Lori said she was ready for for a shower and bed. Once in bed, I was almost asleep when Lori asked why we needed any more money? Lori asked what we would do with more money? I again promised that once we chased the Soviets and Cubans from Nicaragua and got rid of Noriega I would settle down.

The next morning I called Bob and told him I could't make it to the brunch tomorrow but I could do it today and that he was invited to the Island wedding. Bob couldn't make either of my offers but said he was free the following weekend.

I would call Ted, we would meet for lunch. Ted said that the girl, who was only 14 had started talking once she was hungry and ate. Ted said that they had enough to bring in Noriega for questioning but, that he had gone back to Panama yesterday afternoon. Ted then also mentioned the matter of diplomatic immunity that Noriega would most certainly use. The girl, Ted said, hadn't seen her parents since they were taken away from their house some weeks ago. The girl said that Noriega himself had come to her school and picked her out. The girl said they drove me to my house and took my father and mother into custody for no reason other than they were my parents. Noriega told her that depending on how she treated him, he would one day soon release her parents. Ted said it sounded terrible but that how it's done when you live under a dictatorship. Ted said the state department was looking for the girls family.

Ted gave me some bad news about Tim with the Daily News, Ted said that, Tim had gone into hiding with his family from all the threats he was receiving from the articles that he had written about the drug trade that was coming from Columbia then through Panama. The last straw was a car had come by and sprayed Tim's house with bullets. Tim and the family weren't home and no one was hurt but, Ted said you can imagine how Tim's wife felt when she found out. I then told Ted to arrange it to move Tim and family to my Mandeville house. I said to set it up that Tommy did the transport. I wasn't sure how many guards were at the house in Mandeville, but if not enough we would move whatever was needed. Ted said he had told Tim that we would think of something. I said to tell Tim that after his wife stayed there a while he'd have to find a better paying job. Ted had seen and visited the Mandeville house when he had assisted with our first two C-130s deliveries to the airport there.

I up dated Ted about our latest trip to San Andrés and our meeting with Morales. Ted asked if I thought we could trust Morales? I said no. I informed Ted that I had given the green light to restart recon flights off the coast of Columbia starting next week.

Lori and I would leave for Nassau from her today's swim practice. Salinas had invited us to stay at Hill Top but Lori said we should stay at Deanna's beach house.

It was strange how things had changed, Lori mentioning Deanna's beach house when she hadn't even heard the old stories of Michelle, Deanna, and me. I wondered how they, meaning Salinas, Christina and Lori would have got on together with Michelle and Deanna. Michelle would have now been 40 years old if she had lived, Deanna 36. Deanna's sister Janie was now 34 and had three children with Lee. I imagined that Salinas had heard the stories from Betty that I had taken Janie to live with me in Miami when she was only 16 or 17, I couldn't remember. I knew that I had put her in the same High School that Lori was attending. When Janie graduated I sent her off to Florida State where she met Lee. Betty and Janie were the only ones that knew the complete story. Angee would also know a great deal of the history as would Willy. Willy I though, I would have to sit with him this weekend.

I was day dreaming, Lori kissed me and told me to come back. I looked at her and realized that here I was with this beautiful young girl. Through the Leer window I could see the Northern tip of Andros. Again that view took me back to when Rusty and I first sailed east around the northern end of the Island. Jim, Lori said come back to me. I again looked at her and she kissed me. Lori said what I needed was a good hot shower. I could have gone right back to daydreaming but Lori took my left hand and put it on her stomach and said to talk to my unborn son. What will be his name Lori asked? If it's a boy his name will be Gary I said. And if it's a girl Lori asked? Joe-Anne if that's alright I asked? That will be just fine Lori said, Gary or Joe-Anne.

CHAPTER XI

BACK TO NASSAU

We were now landing in Nassau, it was good to be here. It was almost dark and we were picked up by none other than Malcolm, Wendy Michelle, and Carolina. Malcolm hugged Lori; while the girls came to me, Wendy Michelle called me Papa with Carolina, unsure what to call me. I hugged Carolina and said welcome to the family, I looked at her and said Papa would do just fine. I got a good handshake and hug from Malcolm, and with Malcolm holding Lori's hand, Wendy Michelle, and Carolina had mine, as we walked.

Once at the beach house, Malcolm and the girls departed, saying they'd see us tonight at dinner. Malcolm said both girls would go out pulling traps with him and Otis tomorrow morning.

Lori and I would have our shower and be driven back to town. We first stopped at the City Bar and there was Willy waiting. Willy now up there in age said he had only came in because he knew I was coming. I hugged Willy like never before. Willy asked Lori if I was slowing down and of course Lori said I was worst than ever. Willy laughed and started telling stories. Willy said it was his favorite pass time, telling the stories. Willy said he used to tell bits and pieces but that now days people just didn't believe the stories unless he started from the beginning. Willy said he remembered it all. Willy looked at me and said that we had a few bad moments but that all in all it was mighty fine, yes mam mighty fine. Willy said that he now got crawfish or a grouper every day delivered to the house.

Lori and I didn't stay long; we were meeting the gang at the Bahamian Cuisine for dinner.

This was the pre-wedding dinner, Lori was dressed to kill. Lori asked a favor of me before we walked in? Lori said she wanted me to kiss and hug Christina. Close your eyes and believe it's me she said. I asked why, she said it was the right thing to do. You still only will have two wives and I trust you will only kiss her. I smiled and said that she wasn't to leave my side. Lori said not to worry.

At dinner that night, It was hard for me to swallow when Wendy Michelle and Carolina walked in, especially since Wendy Michelle was attached to Malcolm. I hardly recognized many of the group. They had all gotten older. It was the first time I saw Fernando in a suit, he was quite handsome. Christina came in and I did hug and kiss her, with her whispering in my ear. Salinas would be the last to arrive at the dinner. As she walked in, she reminded me of Michelle, not the looks but everyone in the room knew she was the Queen of Nassau. It was now Salinas that owned the town. Salinas wore a long black dress with that small waist and well you know. The dress was a low cut with long sleeves. The thin gold belt, diamond bracelet and diamond neckless sparkled as did her beautiful dark brown eyes. Salinas's hair was up and showed those big diamond ear rings with a diamond crown in her hair. With Lori hanging on my arm Salinas came right at me, hugging me and kissing me, then doing the same to Lori. Salinas then turned to the crowd and announced that Lori was now carrying a child in her belly. Everyone applauded. Everyone was there except for Jack, Jobe, and Evette. Jack was busy keeping us safe while Tommy was coming in with Evette, Jobe and I hoped, Jena.

The get together was started with champagne and me giving a short speech about how our family had grown. Fernando and Maria now beginning as a Family within our Family. As I finished up, in came Evette, Jobe and yes, Jena too. Salinas then stood and talked about the children, soon Salinas said the docks, beaches, air and waters of the Bahamas will be full of this groups next generation of young people. Salinas then looking at Maria said for Maria to listen up. Our children will one day be doing what we do, catching crawfish, assisting the tourist in having a better vacation and of course, taking their money. Everyone laughed. Salinas then said she wanted only one change for our children. I don't want them to be a part of the adventure of war. There are plenty of dangers such as sharks and treacherous waters here. Please gentlemen, looking at me, then said and women. Let's get out of the business of war. The group then applauded, then Salinas said if you men are looking for adventure us women can provide it for you. Then the women applauded and the men better have as I did.

Dinner and the night flew by. I was sure that Salinas was going to come home with us but she did not. She too whispered in my ear. As we all started leaving, I saw Carolina go with Salinas and saw Malcolm and Wendy Michelle walking hand and hand toward the docks. Lori also had my hand and we were walking a half a block behind them. Lori asked what I was thinking? I said I was thinking of getting her on the Hunter. Not that she said, what about those two she asked? Lori reminded me that she was only 15 when I took her to Manila. I said that Wendy Michelle's mother Deanna was also 15 at the time I had met her. I wanted to call out to them but I did not, I stopped and kissed Lori and told her I loved her. As we walked, I noticed that Malcom had turned in at the City Docks, by the time we did the same, they were gone. All 4 of our boats were docked as there were no tourist trips tonight. I stopped and watched for a light to come on in one of the boats but that didn't happen. Lori and I walked to the end of the dock, but no sign of Malcolm and Wendy Michelle. Lori made the comment, a touch of the captain. We walked back to the Hunter and I hoped that the cabin door wasn't locked from the inside. Once in the Hunter's cockpit Lori turned on lights. She stepped down into the cabin and dropped her dress on the floor.

I was up and out before day light heading to Hill Top. No I wasn't going for that, I was going to she if Wendy Michelle had come home. When I arrived Betty was up and coffee was ready. I first checked Wendy Michelle's bed. There she was still asleep. When I turned there was Salinas saying that I needed a shower. In that great shower, I asked about Malcolm and Wendy Michelle. Salinas said she was sure they were lovers, and that yes Wendy Michelle had been to the good Doctor and that she had talked to Wendy Michelle about sex. How did that go I asked? I told her that if Malcom was the one, she should keep him close not allowing him to want for anything. I told her of my mistake of leaving you and how much it had cost me. Wendy Michelle will be just fine Salinas said, they make a good couple, its Carolina that I worry about Salinas said. Wendy Michelle is Carolina's lifeline, but Carolina also has a crush on Malcolm. Enough talk Salinas said, kiss me.

After a short time at Hill Top, I caught the same ride to the docks as Wendy Michelle and Carolina. When we arrived, Lori was with Malcolm and Otis on one of the newest boats. This boats name was "Maggie". Good morning I said stepping aboard. Lori coming to kiss me said she figured where I had gone but wasn't sure.

Lori had that black bathing top on and had found one of the girls shorts on the Hunter. Lori said she'd like to go out with the boat and I could spend some time with the children. Otis looked at me and said she would be fine. The girls came aboard and I kissed Lori and I stepped off. As I watched them and the other boats leave, I then heard an old familiar downshift. As I turned it was Salinas driving with big belly. Yes, it was Salinas and Christina in Michelle's old MG. It was a sight seeing Christina getting herself out of that small MG. Salinas asked how I liked it. I said that Twenty years ago it was fine because there was less traffic but I didn't want her driving that thing around because it was to small and had no protection. I asked if Carlos our mechanic had check it and cleared it for them to drive? Salinas said that Carlos had ordered new tires.

The girls invited me for breakfast at Angee's, instead, I would grab a bite from one of Angee's food carts and head for Hill Top to spend the day with the children. When I arrived Jena was already there. Aunt Jena as she told the children to call her was ready for the pool. Jena said she was glad to see me without the girls. Jena said she wanted to show me her appreciation for the invite. Jena's thank you, would be limited to a small kiss in front of the children that Johnny said he was going to tell his mama. Jena looked good for her age. I couldn't figure her being with that no good. I knew better than anyone that she didn't need the money. At the house the children were happy to play and swim with Papa. We all had a great day of it with Salinas and Christina showing up at about noon. The five kids and even Salinas's two assistants played in the pool or on the beach. Jena would leave early, the wedding was scheduled for 8:00 p.m. at the Methodist church. Fernando nor Maria were Methodist but that was the church they chose.

At about 4:00 p.m. I would head down to the fisherman's wharf to see the boats come in. The "Defiance" had returned from its day trip and was being cleaned. I climbed the Defiance's tuna tower with a pair of binoculars and spotted the "Maggie" heading in. Looked more like play than work. All three girls were on the bridge and I could see Malcom climbing up the latter with a bucket of water. I knew their screams couldn't be heard from here but I knew they were screaming and laughing. We had 5 boats out today, the "Johnny", "Michelle", "Princess" "Pirate" and our newest "Maggie" all of the band came in with a good catch. I was having so much fun watching, so I just stayed there until Captain Mike spotted me and came on up with two cold beers. Captain Mike's beer brand was anything cold. Two cold beers coming up he said as he climbed the ladder. Mike asked if he had to ware something special to the wedding. I looked at him and said he was good to go as he was. If I would have told him anything different he would have used that as an excuse not to go at all. Soon one of the crew notice Mike and I and yelled to come on down. Malcolm and Otis were still throwing cold water. I was sure that water was coming from the crawfish pools. Lori would have a time washing the crawfish smell from her hair for the wedding. I claimed down and Lori met me at the bar. Willy was there waiting with two Polly girls. Lori was not a beer drinker but took a swig to please Willy. Otis brought in Willy's crawfish and Willy thanked him. This is my boy Willy said, he always remembers his uncle Willy. I hadn't noticed before now, but Malcolm had shipped his BMW over here. It had to be one of the nicest cars on the Island. It also had to smell like crawfish. I could think of worse things.

The crowd would thin, Lori and I would head to the beach house, shower and get ready. The after-wedding party for the guest would be at Willy's.

The wedding went off like a wedding should, not to many words except I do and I do and it was over. Tommy was at the wedding and was ready to take Fernando and Maria where ever they were headed, the Honeymoon was on me.

Willy's was full with an open bar that extended out on the dock. Those that were involved in the night time tourists trips would have to pass on the party as their two boats would be leaving at 9:00 p.m. sharp. The "Defiance" would not be going out tonight as both cruise ships would be departing at about 2:00 a.m. The tourist that were going out with our boats tonight were either staying at our boarding houses or at the Holiday Inn on Paradise Island.

Lori and I had planed to take the "Defiance" and head on over to the old treasure circle and anchor for the night. Captain Mike would have the night off.

Lori and I left the dock at about 11:00 p.m. The "Defiance" was huge for just the two of us, Lori cast off all the lines and the both of us sat up on the bridge and slowly pulled out of the dock into the current that was moving east at a pretty good lick. I told Lori about the first time that Rusty and I had come into the dock that first morning with the tide moving in the same direction. I then switched and started telling her of my boyhood, how I always worked for my money and then spent it on one adventure or another. Camping, sailing, fishing and even building our first fort on one of the barrier Islands just off the Coral Reef Yacht Club. I told her that a storm was coming and us kids; my friends and I tried to talk my dad into letting us stay in the fort during the on coming storm. Of course my dad said no because I was here tonight telling the story. After the storm passed my dad took us down to the bay line and showed us that not only was our fort not there any more, the Island had shrunk down to almost nothing. Surely if we would have stayed there we would have been washed away by the storm.

Lori liked hearing my stories and before we knew it we had arrived at the treasure circle. Lori took the wheel and I dropped anchor.

Lori and I had a nice little break and were back the next day in time for us to catch the Chalk's afternoon seaplane to Miami. Years back, everyone at the small seaplane base knew me; I was always late and smelled like fish or crawfish.

When we arrived to the apartment in Miami there was a note on the door that let us know our neighbor was here. Jena had left the note saying to call or knock on the door. I figured that I'd give her a call after Lori went to school the next day. Jena and I could go for lunch.

In our shower Lori said how much she enjoyed the trip and admitted that before going she wasn't looking forward to it. She said, she appreciated how I handled things with Christina. Lori said her best time was pulling traps with the other girls, Malcolm and Otis. Lori said she could do that everyday. I said that would change in another few months. Lori said that we'd be going back for another wedding soon. She wasn't sure when but said that Wendy Michelle noted that Malcolm had said they would marry once he was the captain of his own boat. Well I said, Malcom still had the money in the bank that his Grandfather had left him. Then I thought about the other thing, Malcolm's parents. There goes more bad mouthing Captain Jim again I said out loud.

Lori then said that Salinas was enjoying her life without being pregnant. Lori said that Salinas said that we should come visit more often and that the next time you went fishing that she should pack a small bag and come on over and stay at the the Hill Top house. Lori said that she knew that Salinas planned on taking advantage of the situation once she has gotten further along with her pregnancy. I knew exactly what she meant by taking advantage.

CHAPTER XII

THE WORST OF NEWS

The next morning Lori was off to school and I was knocking on Jena's door when our house girl came out to the hallway and said there was a urgent call for me. It was just after 10:30 a.m. when I reached and picked up the phone. Salinas and Christina had been in a terrible car accident! It was bad, both girls were said to be on the way to the hospital. Lourdes said she had just received the call from Janie and said that her information was that there had been at least one death. I asked where Tommy was and she said he should be in Miami, I said that I'd be at the airport in twenty minutes. As I ran by Jena's door she had it open and chased me into the elevator.

By the time we reach the airport and was in the cockpit, Lourdes was on the phone again saying that there were no survivors. Salinas and Christina had died in the accident!

I walked off the airplane and started for a taxi, I turned and yelled to Tommy to be on stand by that I would return with Lori. I caught a taxi and went to the school, walking into the office to ask where to find Lori. The office gave me a room number and I went to it's door. Lori saw me at the door and knew it was something bad. Lori and I stepped out into the hall and holding her in my arms told her of the accident. We held each other while crying, she kept saying that it couldn't be true it just couldn't be. We then walked out to our waiting taxi. We didn't say much, Lori's arm was trembling as she held me. We arrived at the Leer, Jena was still there waiting. We took off and within the hour we're landing in Nassau. Lourdes had called and said that Salinas's and Christina's bodies were located at the morgue. We went straight there and I was the only one that was allowed back in to see the bodies. Both body's were badly mangled, the morgue not as yet even being able to notice that Christina had been more than 6 months pregnant. Both bodies were unrecognizable but it was clear, it was them.

I walked out thinking about the children. We would then go from the morgue to the house. Betty was there with the children, only Wendy Michelle, Carolina and Johnny had figured out what was going on. I asked if Sharron, Salinas's mom had been called and I was told she had. I then put a call into Sharron to confirm the tragic news and tell her that I would send Tommy for her.

The phone didn't stop ringing, most were calling because they had heard about the accident and didn't know how bad it was.

Lori and Jena were helping out with the smallest children as for them it was, at least for now just another day.

I started making arrangements for the funeral, Salinas would be buried here in Nassau and I wasn't even sure about Christina's family, where they lived or for that matter their names.

Salinas's funeral would be the next afternoon at the Methodist church that we had just been to for Saturday's wedding.

The MG had been moved to the police station for the investigation. I went to see it, it was just a ball of steel and blood. The left front tire was blown, Deanna's father now retired, met me there to take a look. The preliminary report said that Salinas was driving around the curve and the front left tire could have blown out causing Salinas to lose control. The car rolled and hit a large pine tree at the top center of the car, folding the car around the tree. There was no surviving that crash and no suffering involved. Mr. Johnson and I then went to see our mechanic, Carlos. Carlos was still in his office, he was sitting with the tears still rolling down his face. He was looking at the paper that he had Salinas sign for the MG. When he saw my face he stood and tearfully said this was all his fault. I told her Senior Jim, I told her that the tires were dry rotted and she should wait until new tires came from the mainland. I wrote it down on the receipt that she signed for the car. Maybe she didn't understand the danger Carlos said. This is all my fault he said again, I just should have stood my ground and said no to her.

By late that night, people starting showing up for the funeral, Salinas's mom had arrived and was with the children. Wendy Michelle, Carolina and Johnny had been taken out of school with the news, both girls had now gone and sat on the dock waiting for Malcolm's return from pulling traps. From the docks with Malcolm and others, the girls came back to the house. The house was a mess with lots of people, Lori didn't want to even enter Salinas's room not to mention sleep in her bed. Lori and I got some pillows and would try to get some sleep out on the porch. It had been a while since I talked to Lori about life's choices. I told Lori that Carlos the mechanic had told Salinas that the tires on the MG were dry rotted and that she should wait until the new ones came from Miami. Lori wasn't there when I told Salinas and Christina that I didn't like them in that small car because it had no protection in case of an accident. Carlos made a bad choice, I too could have, should have stopped them on Saturday. Salinas also made a bad choice, a choice she never realized that would end up killing them. I hate it I said, but I'm mad with her for leaving us as she did. Please remember about the choices, I said. Now, you will be making choices for yourself and others.

Lori did get to sleep, me I went and checked on the children; Betty and one of the Haitian girls were in one room with the two youngest boys while Jena, Malcolm, Wendy Michelle, Carolina, Johnny, Michelle, Kelly, and the other Haitian girl were all sleeping in another room. From there I walked out to the beach to think. Lori at 17 was awful young to be thrown into being the mother of eight. She had chosen to have one baby saying and thinking she'd have this one and still finish high school. I thought about it over and over. June wasn't here as yet but she had called and said she was on the way. There was a possibility, a slim one, but it was a possibility that I could live with, but could she, would she and would Lori agree? The other possibility was Jena, here it wouldn't be whether she would say yes, here she would want to get married and have a child of her own. At some point I thought Jena would get those itchy feet and run, leaving us with another baby for someone to take care of. Then there were the two Haitian girls that had been with Salinas for over a year now.

Seems the sun had started up before I got a wink of sleep. As I was heading up the stairs to the porch, Lori was standing there waiting for me. As I took that last step up, she hugged me and again started with the crying. Lori then said that she would quit school and come take care of the children. I told her that I would make that call and she would need to live with whatever I needed to do. Lori then said she'd rather have June than Jena. Lori said she didn't want either but at least she new that June didn't need to have anymore children. Lori looked at me and said whatever I decided she would abide by. Lori had thought it before I had said it. Next out of the kitchen came Wendy Michelle and Malcolm; Wendy Michelle said that she and Malcolm could marry and take care of the children. Then Jena was right behind them saying she would move in and take care of the children. Then Carolina, she said she would take care of and raise the children. Then there was Betty that said that whomever was going to take these children would be filling some awfully big shoes and what they would really need was a father that stayed close to home. Then it was Sharron's turn to say she would take Salinas's three back with her.

We were all eating breakfast when the taxi pulled up. It was June with our daughter Kayla. We all saw the taxi driver open the trunk and pull out, and put on the ground those three large suit cases.

June then, with Kayla in hand walked up to me and introduced my daughter to her father.

June then looked around, then looked back at Lori and said hello little sister and came and hugged her. Then it was on to Wendy Michelle. Wendy is that you June asked? Yes mam Wendy said. Then she spotted Malcolm and said, you must be Carson's boy. Malcolm looked at June and said yes, mam. Then June spotted Jena and went and they hugged. I think everyone noticed there was no hug for me. Betty was right up there too, with Betty telling one of the men to put Ms. June's things in Salinas' room. By now all the little ones were up, June asking which one was which. June just about ignored me altogether. At first I thought that what I had thought about was going to be out of the question.

The phone was like grand central station. I had calls from all over including Brian, Brian's grandfather, the CIA Director, the Admiral, Liz, several people from G.D. and I even got a call from the First Lady.

I had decided to have Christina's body cremated and would take it back to the Philippines. I had not ever visited Joe-Anne's grave in Manila but would now do so. Joe-Anne's death now hit me again as this brought back so much of the pain. I had not looked at the deaths before, but I thought how many people close to me had died.

The Funeral was scheduled for 4:00 p.m. Janie and her mom were in charge. Lori went to the beach house and picked out clothes for the both of us to wear to the funeral.

Before I knew it I was standing in front of a larger than life crowd that filled the church and the outside street well into the park. I tried to speak but the words got stuck in my throat. All of a sudden it hit me that Salinas was gone. I wept as the words slowly came out. Salinas was a dedicate wife and mother, a friend to all, she constantly gave and gave never asking anything for herself. We, myself and the children, friends and family will all miss her. We love you Salinas I said, I love you. From there I could hardly make it back to my seat, my legs wobbled like when I had been underwater, short on air, digging up treasure too long. Lori was there waiting for me to sit and hold me.

When the service was over we carried Salinas's casket out and buried her next to Deanna.

From there many of the large crowd walked down to the city bar. The bar had been closed during the funeral but Willy was now there serving. Once opened, the bar had standing room only. I led the first toast. We will never forget you.

My heavy emotion was now over and I had arrived back to reality, I then started seeing faces like Bob's, Jena, Lourdes, Jerry, Cindy, Tim, Joan, Evette, Jack, Jody, Robin, Montibelli, Dan, Tim and Ida, Mark and Lisa, Otis and Maggie, Angee, Deanna's mom and dad, Janie and Lee, Richard, Madalyn and Charles, Mrs. King, Diane and Marco and others. The entire time Lori held my arm and didn't let go. From the bar we all walked down and I dropped a reef into the out going tide. We stood and watched as it disappeared into the harbor. As I turned with Lori still latched on to me., there she was with her arms open. It was June, she had stayed with the children during the funeral. June stepped right in and with a strong hug said that she would be staying if that would be ok. Then June looked at Lori and asked if that was going to be ok with her. Lori then joined the hug.

Now walking back up the dock, I had two women, one on each arm.

Most of the people didn't stay the night, they were returning on late afternoon or evening flights. The crawfish traps weren't pulled that day but the tourist did go out that night. Lori and I would again spend the night on the porch at Hill Top. Tonight we had little miss Kayla come looking for me every few minutes with Jimmy and Jacques following her every move.

It was almost daylight, today I was hoping for Lori and me to be leaving, making a short stop in Miami and then on to Manila with Christina's ashes. First I would need to settle what would happen here with June.

I was up knocking on June's door at 5:00 a.m., funny I hadn't realized that either I had lost my robe or June had brought one just like the ones I had in my Miami apartment. June opened the door with that familiar robe on and said that it was too early and for me to go away. June had opened the door then closed it again. I again knocked and told her to put on some clothes that I needed to talk to her. June opened the door again and said that we didn't need to talk about it. June said she was staying and that was it. I'm going to raise our daughter with her brothers and sisters she said. I'm here where I belong she said and again shut the door.

I then again headed for the beach. I was walking east when I turned and saw someone walking my way. I stopped and waited, it was June. I asked, you didn't marry the guy? June said no. Why not I asked? Well she said it just didn't feel right and it would have been my second mistake.

June said Salinas had called her several times asking her to come and visit or even stay. June said in the last couple months she and Salinas had talked quite a bit. She loved you Jim, June said, but said you were not her's and she felt you never would be. She said that she and I were alike. Salinas said one day you would return and live here and we would all be together. Salinas asked if I loved you, I told her yes from the very first time I had met you. Salinas said that it was the same with her. Salinas said she wasn't sure that you loved her, but she was sure you would never leave her. Kayla needs a father and I need a man, a real man June said. While your in the house my door will never be locked she said, but please, don't wait to long to come to me. June took my arm and we headed back toward the house. Lori was there at the porch door. As we walked up the stairs, June said it was all worked out. June said to Lori, you are the primary and I am secondary. I'll take of the children and you study. June walking by Lori said to please take Jena with us when we left, she then turned and said she would have only one rule, then said two. No girlfriends and when visiting Nassau we both sleep here. Looking at me, June said she would need at least two more rooms to be added to the present house and a tennis court. June stepped forward toward me and gave me a small kiss, turned and walked back to her bedroom. Well, I said looking at Lori, what do you think? Lori without a smile, said she'd like to see her in a bathing suit before giving an opinion. I stepped in and kissed her.

Lori knew we would be traveling to Manila and General Santos. We would be stopping in Miami to pick up what needed for the trip. We offered a ride to Jena but she said she would stick around to see how things worked out.

Lori said that having me all to herself would be something that she would like but that having 7 or 8 children and taking care of me could become a challenge.

Once in Miami the hot shower was the same if not better than ever.

Once I checked the computer, I saw that Jack had been busy, not only had he watched over us in Nassau but also watched Paix. Jack had sent one of our C-130 to pick up two replacement Lasers for Paix. That C-130 had also brought in two more rifle stile Lasers.

Fernando was out of touch since their wedding night and they most likely hadn't even heard of the accident. Jack had his bird parked at Andros and had flown on in to Nassau to be with Cindy. Jack said that Cindy had grown close to Salinas.

Lori and I decided to wait until December to return Christina's ashes to the Philippines. Lori would go to school tomorrow while I would visit Roy and once again change my will. Lori didn't go to swim practice, she said she didn't want to leave me alone. Lori said for some reason she was feeling heavy. I guess so, I said you are almost three months pregnant.

Again that night Lori said she was worried what June would look like in a bathing suit. I told Lori that June was about the same age as she was when I met her, it was the summer of 1968. June was as Skinny as a rail and falling out of her bathing suit top. I stopped and thought about those times, I was still 16 at the time and having two a day football practices. On Saturday's we only had one morning practice. The chalk's flight would leave for Nassau at 3:30 p.m. After a Saturday's morning practice, I had time to kill so I had gone down to the sailing club to bail the rain water out of the "Princess". June, my Cousin Clair and some of the other sailing club girls were there at the club washing cars. To get my attention, June had stuck the water hose down the back of my pants. Back then, before football practice started, I had just spent most of the summer in Nassau sharing a boarding house room with Deanna. Wow I thought, that was 21 years ago. Seemed like yesterday.

Lori's kiss would bring me back to the reality at hand. I was in love with a beautiful young girl of 17 years old, she is my wife and she is three months pregnant. Just less than 200 miles to the east, south east I now have 8 children living under one roof, with an old girl friend which is the mother of one of the eight which is now the primary care giver to all of my children. Five of the children are mine while three were adopted. Lori's will be my sixth child bringing my total, including the three adopted children to nine.

The next morning Lori would go to school, with me telling her I would see her at swim practice. I told her that if she wanted to excel in her swimming she would have to do so with xtra effort.

That morning we received a heads up on a large shipment of drugs that would be leaving from Columbia going to Cuba, I though it strange, and asked myself why Cuba? The answer came in a phone call asking me to fly up and meet with the Director. Today was Friday and I wasn't planning to miss another day with Lori so we made arrangements to meet for a late dinner that would take place in Boston. The Director asked that Jack be up in the air ready to move if I so agreed to stop the drugs from arriving to their destination. The Director said that he was coming with a friend, I said I'd be coming up with Lori.

I went to Lori's practice, she worked hard. Lori had told her coach and friends that she had missed practice because a family member of mine had passed away in a car accident.

I was wondering when the coach would notice Lori's belly and what she would say. Surely Lori's teammates would see the difference in the locker room.

When I told Lori we were going to Boston, she said she would stop on the way home and visit the Latin girls at the hair salon. I reminded her that our dinner was set for 10:00 p.m and we needed to be at the Leer by 6:00 p.m. Lori said she'd call me from the stylist and if she was

going to be running behind, she'd have the house girl pack her a bag.

As it went, I would be meeting Lori at the Leer. Lori met us there, I thought it odd that she had her hair in a pony tail.

Once in the air Lori spent quite a bit of time getting ready. I was in my usual black suit and Lori, her hair now dried and curled with her beautiful red evening dress, Lori looked supper.

At the restaurant we met the Director and Liz. What an odd couple I thought. Both the Director and Liz again gave their condolences for both Christina and of course Salinas.

We weren't sitting two minutes before Liz asked Lori how far along she was, Lori looking at me said three months. Congratulations are in order the Director said. We then ordered our food and Liz invited Lori to the ladies room.

The Director said that the plane from Columbia was loading the drugs as we spoke. The cargo would be headed to Cuba with a return cargo of updated arms for the FARC. The mission, the Director said was to disorient the Cuba bound plane's navigation for it to be lost a sea. The plane, the Director said was not to reach Cuba. I was given a GPS location and a departure time of midnight tonight. I said that Lori and I would have to take a rain check for the dinner as my only way of communication with Jack was the computer on board the Leer. Lori came back with Liz and I stood and excused Lori and myself. I asked the Director if he could ride with Lori and myself back to the airport. Liz asked if she too could ride with us. All four of us walked out, Liz telling the waiter to put this on her tab. During our ride to the airport we used paper and pen to communicate. I wrote them both, why not get rid of Noriega? And why wouldn't the Colombian government just arrest Morales and even Escobar. Liz wrote that Noriega worked for the CIA, the Director wrote, that was not true. I wrote to Liz, what does Noriega do for the CIA? Liz wrote it's not what he does, it's what he has done in the past. I wrote, he knows to much. Liz wrote, exactly. I wrote who is protecting him? Liz wrote back, the Vice President. I wrote back, does the President know? Liz wrote back, yes. I wrote Liz back asking again about Escobar. The Director wrote back that the opposition controlled the Senate in Columbia and was financed by

Escobar. Escobar also was said to have several Generals and most of the police in the rebel held territories on his payroll.

Before I knew it we were parked along side Tommy's Leer. I got out of the limo and asked if they were still friends? Liz said they were friends with a much different political view. We all said our goodbyes. As the limo pulled away I thought, what was the possibility that they were lovers?

CHAPTER XIII

TESS TAKES ON CUBA'S MIGS

Once Lori and I were in the Leer, I used the computer to contact Jack. It was almost midnight when I got back into the cabin, Lori had pulled down the fold-out bed and gone to sleep. I made sure she was buckled in and went back to the cockpit. We were cleared for take-off and up in the air within moments.

On the way to Miami, we kept getting updates from Jack. Jack now had the two engine cargo plane on radar and satellite, it would be within TESS's control range within moments. We received a message that the C-130's satellite now picked up two then four of what TESS marked in as MiGs coming in from Cuba. Jack's next message requested permission to in-gage. I sent him word that the mission stood.

We were in the air on the way to Miami when we received several messages. Jack had reported that our C-130 had the cargo plane within the 100 mile mark and had TESS messing with their navigation and electrical. The cargo plane now without navigation, having a heading of what would, at the moment put them making landfall at the southwestern coast of Texas.

The four MiGs must have know about the C-130's capabilities because even before they came into our 100 mile radius they spilt up to cover a wider area. The C-130 could hear the MiG pilots talking saying that once they located the C-130 they were to hit the C-130 with everything they had. As the MiGs entered into the TESS radius. Jack had messaged that one of the MiGs could come within visual contact within minutes.

By now our Leer was on a descent to the Opa-Locka airport, I was anxiously waiting for the next message.

The messages now flowing in said that a MiG had fired two missiles that TESS had knocked down. The MiG then came back around with what looked to be a machine gun or Kamikaze run. With the MiG's missiles armed and the MiG heading at the C-130, TESS fired twice. The shots took out the remaining missiles, their disintegration took down the MiG. Our C-130 still following the cargo plane, which had made a circular movement showing just how confused they were. Clearly the cargo plane had no idea where they were but, the other three MiGs would have seen the blast from the destroyed MiG and were heading in our C-130's general direction.

Cuba hearing the news that they had lost one MiG dispatched two more.The MiGs still in TESS's range had no navigation but wouldn't need it to find our C-130. The messages then stopped for ten minutes then started back again. The message said that TESS had knocked down three more MiGs and was still traveling about two miles behind the cargo plane. Jack also messaged that Cuba had called back the last two MiGs that they had put up. Jack said that someone must have figured that the cargo plane was doomed do to a lack of fuel. Jack's last message was that they had moved within visual contact and watched as one man threw out what Jack thought was a life raft then the three crew parachuted out the door. Jack said the cargo plane flew another five miles then took a dive into the ocean. Jack noted that it was dark and they would not be able to assist the cargo plane's crew but had noted their GPS location, our mission was accomplished, and our C-130 would be heading home.

Our leer would be on the tarmac hearing Jack's last communication. I would wake Lori and having two cars there, Lori would drop off her BMW at the apartment and we would have breakfast at the Brickell Town House. From there, Lori wanted to spend the day sailing on the Morgan. We stopped at Big Daddy's for Robert's pint of Jim Beam and Scotty's as I was sure once out there on the water Lori wouldn't want to come back in.

Lori still looking good in her red evening dress again she made still another impression on the sailing club's Robert. I wasn't sure which Robert was licking his lips over, the Jim Beam or my wife. Either way Lori liked Robert's attention.

We sailed all day with mostly Lori at the wheel, we had gone through a good rain shower that cooled us off. We were out on the ocean side of Key Largo and for sure weren't going to make it back tonight. Lori came about, and with the wind behind us, we started up the bar-b-q as we headed north. At about midnight, we anchored just off the old lighthouse on Key Biscayne. We were anchored just off the shallows at the lighthouse. As the sun started up we moved the boat closer to shore, anchored and swam in. Lori seamed a bit more secure in her conversations. She was more relaxed and talked more than ever about plans. Lori said she wanted me out of the spy business as she called it. She also said that every time she closed her eyes she saw June in a bathing suit looking good while she was with her big belly. Lori said she wasn't sure we had made the right decision about the kids. I said, you mean June. Lori said yes.

We got back to the apartment at about 6:00 p.m. There were lots of messages from everyone from the White House, the Admiral, Bob, June, Malcolm, Lee, Jena, the Director, and of course, Liz. It was Sunday night, and the house girl said the phone hadn't stopped ringing.

My first call was to June, I think Lori was hoping that maybe June had changed her mind. No such luck, June was calling about Wendy Michelle and Malcom. June said that Malcolm had gone fishing with Wendy Michelle on Saturday night and did not return until about noon today. June said she had spoken to them both, Wendy Michelle saying she was going to move in with Malcolm. June said that Carolina said that if Wendy Michelle went, she too was going with Wendy Michelle. June asked that I come and talk to all three of them. I asked to speak to Wendy Michelle and told her that she would not miss an hour of school and that I'd be there this week to talk to her and Malcolm. Wendy Michelle was quick to say that she had heard from her aunt Janie that both Deanna and Janie had lived with me when they were her age. Yes I said and neither of them missed any school. I then said that if they expected my approval they would wait until I got there to talk about it. Wendy Michelle then said that they would wait. June then came back on the phone and I said to talk to her about not getting pregnant. June asked when I would be visiting; I said I should be there this week. I then called Malcolm and didn't get an answer.

My next call was to the Director, he congratulated me and said that the Soviets had a satellite positioned over the site as to watch over the mission. He asked when I could be there to brief the President? The Director mentioned that I could have already gotten a call from the White House. I told him that the Admiral had also called. Yes the Director said, everyone will want a piece of you now he said. I imagined the Soviets were running scared.

I then called Lourdes to locate Jack, Lourdes said that Jack and Cindy were in Miami and said she would have him call me. Then I called Omni Tim to inquire how the Vehicle was doing with our latest test. Tim said he would reply via computer within the next 15 minutes. I called Lee and he said that the Admiral's secretary had called about a new construction project in Homestead Florida.

Jack called and said he could be at the apartment within 30 minutes. I said to come and bring Cindy. Jack showed, but alone. Jack briefed me on the operation. I viewed a consolidated film of most of the action. Jack said that Cindy and he would be getting married in Cindy's home town of Austin Texas in three weeks and of course wanted us there. Jack said that Cindy was wanting, demanding that Jack retire. Jack asked how much notice I would need? Lori hadn't heard what Jack had said and I didn't want her to hear my reply. I told Jack that we were done when the standing President left office. This would give us just a year and three months in. Jack stood and said he was with me, Jack said that once we got out he'd like to go to Boca del Tora and finish our dive of the "Defiance".

I wouldn't call the White House nor the Admiral back until the next morning. Lori went to school the next morning with me saying I be going to Nassau to speak with Wendy Michelle, and Malcolm. I asked her if she was up to traveling to Washington while I met with the powers to be. Lori said she wouldn't want to miss another swim practice but would go if I needed company. Lori meant that if I was thinking of taking anyone she wanted to be the one to go, not June.

The next morning I was out the door at the same time as Lori. Seemed that the habit of my women slapping me on my butt had finally caught up with Lori. Lori said that maybe I should't stay in Nassau over night.

In a way I felt bad about how Lori must have felt but didn't see how this would end up without me having two girls again. A lot would depend on this trip.

I was in Nassau by 8:30 a.m. and at the house by 9:00 a.m. The only children that were in the house were the little ones, the rest were at school. June didn't know I was coming and was bare footed, dressed in a baggy pair of shorts and braw like top. Her hair was short and in good order, she was without makeup and very white. I hadn't looked at her the last time I saw her and this time I noticed she was still a good looking woman, she was 37 years old, some twenty years older than Lori. I was however curious what was under those baggy clothes. To my surprise Jena was still there; to my irritation, Sharron was still there too. June said that Jena was a big help with the kids in the pool. June said that Sharron only spent time with her three grandchildren avoiding the others. June said that Sharron talked badly about how I always mistreated Salinas.

I found Sharron and told her to get her things packed, Sharron said she didn't want to have some strange white person taken care of her grandchildren. I told her she had no say in the matter. Sharron then said she wanted to take over Salinas's property and the trust. I informed Sharron that the old trust having Salinas receiving the money and property had been dissolved and that a new will and trust had been set up for the children. I told Sharron that as long as bearable, she would continue to receive her living allowance plus four yearly visits. Sharron said I was being unfair to her grandchildren, "they are Haitian she stated and should go back with me".

I warned Sharron not to rock the boat that the children were Bahamian and US citizens with no mention of any Haitian bloodline. Sharron knew she would not win any argument here and walked away to pack.

The children were up and around, June asked if I'd like to walk with her on the beach. June now had on flip flops and an old shirt of mine that I hadn't seen in a while. Again I couldn't get a good look at her. We walked down the beach a ways then she stopped and took off my shirt and walked into the water. I got a pretty good look from the back that looked pretty darn good. Then standing in knee deep water she turned and asked if I was coming? When looking, I thought Lori wasn't going to like that, but I certainly did. Under my shorts I had on my speedo, I dropped my shorts and took off the shirt then my side arm, the T shirt and walked on in for that first kiss.

June said that both Wendy Michelle and Carolina would go directly from school to the docks. Both girls worked cleaning our other boats until Otis and Malcolm would come in.

From the beach, I would go down to the docks. I wanted to speak with Malcolm first. Otis and Malcolm came in at right about 4:00 p.m. Only one other boat beat them in. I asked the girls to help Otis while I spoke with Malcolm. Malcolm had gained back all that weight he had lost from his accident and then some. He was a good looking young man that reminded me of his grandfather. His brown hair had turned blond, bleached from the salt water and sun.

Malcolm came right to the point, that if he needed to marry Wendy Michelle, he was ready to. Malcolm said he wanted to use his school money to buy a boat that he, Wendy, and Caroline would work together. He would also sell his Miami house and buy a small beach house here in Nassau. I understand you could stop us sir, but we are in love and want to be together. What about school for the girls I asked? They both have another year and a half I said. They don't want to finish school he said. What about your education I asked? I love it here, Malcolm said, I will live here for the rest of my life. Things change I said. Malcolm said that nothing could change his mind. I then called Wendy Michelle, Carolina started to also come but I signaled to Carolina to stay put. Wendy Michelle I asked, has Malcolm asked you to marry him? We have talked about it, she said. But he hasn't asked, she said. Well if he asks and if you say yes and if you agree to finish high school while married, you both have my blessing. Malcolm, if you wish, I'll find a buyer for your house. Buy a boat that you can fish the west side of Andros. A boat I said that can keep 300 crawfish alive two or three days. What about Carolina Wendy Michelle asked? Carolina can come stay with me and Lori in Miami. That way we'll see how strong your love is for one another. Just the two of you I said. I then said that they should think about it. I then signaled to Carolina and once there I told the girls that curfew on a school night was 10:00 p.m., lights out. Non-school nights 1:00 a.m. and no overnight fishing. We all got this, I asked? They all three said yes sir.

It was now getting dark, I headed on over to see Willy. As I walked in Willy said he'd heard I was in town. Come to see about Wendy Michelle and Malcolm, didn't you, Willy asked? Willy asked if I remembered a young green eyed 15 year old named Deanna? I looked at Willy and said I would always remember those green eyes. I then said that things were different now. Oh said Willy, how so? For one thing, I said, I asked the Constables permission. Willy said, yes you did, if I remember right you baited him, when you had him right where you wanted him, you pulled him right on in and never did take that hook out. I smiled and then Willy and I laughed. As we laughed Willy got serious looking at the door. As I looked in the Mirror it was June. Buy a girl a drink Captain, June asked?

If it hadn't been so soon and it wouldn't have bothered Lori so much, I'd have taken June with me to D.C.

That night the girls, Wendy Michelle and Carolina were in bed with the lights out by ten, all looked like it was under control, I slept on the porch and yes I did check June's door, it was as she said unlocked.

The next morning I was off early for Washington. Lourdes had my trip all planned right down to getting me back to Lori by bedtime.

It was the Admiral first, he said he understood why I this time had come alone. Must be tough losing a wife and mother of so many children, he said.

The Admiral's visit was three fold, first he wanted a date for which we would have the first Vehicle up in the air, second he wanted Lee to start the Homestead project that he had mentioned to Lee and thirdly he wanted both Vehicles moved to Homestead. All of this he wanted now. The Admiral and the President were worried about the Soviets and what they may do to stop our technical advances. The Admiral didn't say it but he was concerned that the Soviets could mount an all out attack on Andros. I thought, maybe even nuclear. The idea was that the Soviets may attack Andros without an all out response by our military, this because the American people didn't know what we had going on there, but they, the Soviets would not attack U.S. soil.

Lee was to start at once getting at least two large Homestead hangers that were now empty, ready for the move. The damaged Vehicle would be moved now and then the first Vehicle moved, hopefully on its own power. I agreed with The Admiral and said that we were very close to a trial run where our C-130 would be used to guide the Vehicle and if that worked out as planned we at that time could move the Vehicle to Homestead or at least get it aboard a carrier. The Admiral laughed at my mention of a carrier saying that a carrier didn't have enough water to get into Homestead.

Of course the Admiral inquired about Karen? I said that unfortunately I had lost contact with her.

Before I left I was told that the Homestead plans were still being drawn up, but Lee should come in and do what he needed with what was already there to receive the cargo.

From the Admiral's office it was to the White House. This time there was no waiting except at the gate where again I was asked to check in my arms.

I was escorted into a briefing room, a first for me, it was the Vice President, not the President that I was meeting with. Seemed that the President was under the weather. These men, except for the Director were a different group of people. I was introduced to them all with the Vice President being quite friendly. I knew that the VP was a decorated war hero that had flown many trips over Germany during the big war. It was said that he was one of only a few that had lost a bomber over Germany and with the resistance made it out only to return piloting a second bomber. The VP looked young for his age and in good shape.

Let's get right to the point the VP said, we have seen what your TESS is capable of and want to start placing it in some of our aircraft. He went on to say that our version of ground Lasers hadn't shown that they were ready for deployment but TESS on the other hand was remarkably unique. One of the other men said, just imagine what a group of our fighters could do with such technology.

Gentlemen, I said, TESS in a fighter was years always and maybe not ever. Don't overlook what powers TESS. TESS in a C-130 takes a two ton battery system that requires a constant recharging of it's system. At present even if you could carry the weight you wouldn't have the space. A cargo plane or and older bomber yes, but a fighter no. The VP then asked why the Vehicle was able to do so much. Well I explained, for one thing we do not know what the Vehicle is capable of. What we do know is it uses two nuclear power rods that are regenerated by electrical power provided by the Vehicle's travel motion or a water pumping device that produces more electrical power than it uses. We have not seen nor have any idea of it's speed, agility or fire power.

A third man asked about the cost, I said that I would be happy to share that with them if I knew.

We are paying for this are we not the VP asked? No sir I said, the President authorized moving $50,000,000.00 of the original $100,000,000.00 congress allotted for the contras. That $50,000,000.00 has gone toward the President's star war project. Who then is funding TESS the VP asked? Myself and G.D. I stated. Why spend anything on a myth like Star Wars when we could have TESS one man asked? Well sir I said, the government has had the ability to act on the technology but that I know of they have not. Then the VP asked about the hand held lasers that he had heard existed. That technology alone would put us way ahead of the Soviets, he said.

I paused then said that I was almost sure the Soviets or the Israelis now had such technology. The VP asked how? I told them all, that I had delivered such a weapon to the White House and apparently it was stolen. Six months after I delivered the laser to the White House, it was delivered to G.D. as part of the Star Wars project and the working components of the laser were missing. The VP asked who attended that meeting? I said the President, and the Secretary of State. The VP said, damn.

I stated that G.D. could provide such a laser but the laser was overweight and thus far untested in battle, again I said, the laser can only fire according to it's electrical charge. To charge the laser after one good shot, it required a charge of 200 amps of 460 volts. This I said is hardly something one would carry into battle.

Your C-130 brought down 4 MiGs did it not? I confirmed that yes this was true. TESS is still being developed. We are learning its capabilities and how it thinks. What do you mean learning how it thinks one man asked? For some reason, I said, TESS has a built in perception of who or what it's enemy is. Do you mean it could react without being programmed too? Yes I said. For instance I said, when any aircraft or ground force picks TESS up on radar TESS knows it's being watched. If that same radar locked on to TESS, depending how TESS perceived the threat, TESS could fire to eliminate the threat. We have made progress but are not sure that TESS wouldn't override our programming. The VP then asked if they, being the government could buy a few units and do some test themselves? I said if you got the money the technology is there. The VP asked how much I had spent. I said it was a privet matter, I have already had some nice experiences with the IRS. The VP then told the others that Uncle Sam had in the past attempted collection of over $2,000,000.00 in taxes from my bank accounts. I added, illegally collected. I then stated that my Uncle Sam now owed me $7,000,000.00 that was to be paid from the $27,000,000.00 that I still had of their money for the contras. You mean to say that of the $100,000,000.00 that was approved over a year ago you still have $27,000,000.00 in the bank. Yes, sir, and $50,000,000.00 of that $100,000,000.00 went to G.D. for Star Wars. The VP asked what I thought about the Star Wars project? I told him that in another 5 years and a billion or two, Star Wars would be up and running. One man said rubbish, while the VP also said that would be a waist of money. The VP then asked about my visit with the Admiral? Then the VP asked, when? I told him that I believed that both Vehicles could be moved within three months.

What about this Haiti facility you are building the VP asked? I said it was being built to have a safe place for TESS to rest? The VP said he had heard my defense wasn't as good as my offense. I said we'd be ready the next time. Will there be a next time the VP asked? Yes sir I said, the Soviets are worried that their military will soon come to the reality that they are out gunned, they will have to try to stop us or obtain the same advantage that we now seem to have. The Director not saying much the entire meeting, said he agreed with my thinking.

When it was over, the Director said he would walk me out, we were stopped and I was asked to follow the young man that had stopped us. The Director said he would wait for me. I was led to the President's residence where I was met by the First Lady. Captain she said, the President is not feeling well but would like to speak to you. He is on medication and may drift some she said. Yes mam I said I understand. I walked in and the President was sitting in bed watching an old cowboy movie. As the President saw me he said Captain, how's that beautiful wife of yours? Cat wasn't it he said. Yes sir I said, the family is doing just fine. Well he said when I get over this dog gone flu we'll have to have dinner again. Yes sir I said. The First Lady then said that the President needed his rest. I told him it was great to see him and that I hoped he'd be feeling better soon. The First Lady then took my hand and escorted me out to the hall where the same young man was waiting. The First Lady apologized for the President and again said he wasn't feeling good.

I told her that if there was anything they needed, all she needed to do was call.

I was led back to where the Director was waiting and we continued walking toward the doors. The Director asked if I had seen the President and how he was? I said the he was sitting reading and seemed fine. Just before we reached the gate I put on a thin pair of gloves, then collected my guns. The Director seemed like he wanted to ask me something so I invited him for the ride to the airport. He accepted without hesitation. In the limo we used paper to communicate. He wrote, they think your hiding something. I wrote, it's not my mistrust. He wrote, with what did the beast knock down those copters and kill the Soviets? I wrote, the beast was very good at rock throwing. I then wrote that our government had discovered and destroyed the being that lived in the first Vehicle. I was hired to bring the Vehicle up. It was delivered intact and complete, all that was taken from the Vehicle by myself was hand delivered to the White House. While in their control they have lost so much, I wrote. The Vehicle's main controller was damaged, caused by a part that had been exchanged while in their possession and control. You heard them, I wrote, they think that Star Wars is a gimmick, it is not. For what they spend on a new carrier, they could have that system up there and working. Your lasers he wrote, where did the technology come from? Ask the Admiral I wrote, it started with what we unearthed on the southern end of Andros. It looked like an electric tooth brush. It was a surgeon's tool. A tool that was used to replace an arm of the leader of a people that had just been attacked by a salt-water crocodile that was over thirty feet long. The Chief, I said had lost has arm fighting what they called the Beast. I continued to write, as we have discovered, that same being had its own Beast to fight, the Beast that we killed two months ago in Nicaragua and the ones that finally destroyed it, mankind.

We arrived at the door of the Leer, I then took out both clips from my guns and handed them to the Director saying one couldn't be to careful these days. I exited the limo, turned and thanked him and said I would keep in touch.

On board I had several extra clips for both guns. I had heard that one of the CIA's new tricks was to put a transponder in the shell where the powder went. One would only find that out if you needed the bullet. Of course that one shell's only use was to provide its location. That possibility wasn't worth taking the chance.

It was early enough that I would get home at a decent hour. Lori would be happy. She would also be happy at the news that Lee would be working a job here very close to Miami.

When I arrived at home I discovered that we had visitors. Wendy Michelle and Carolina were here. The first thing I asked was, if they had missed school today? They both answered at once, no sir. I then asked what about tomorrow's class. The girls had already spoken to Lori and Lori answered for them. They want to go to school here with me. I then asked if June knew they were here. Lori also answered and said that she had called June and told her the girls were here and they were fine. I then asked Lori about my kiss? When I finally got that, I asked the girls what was going on? Wendy Michelle talked and said that both of them were in love with Malcolm and that he couldn't choose. That's why he didn't ask me to marry him, Wendy Michelle said. We told him to chose and he said he couldn't. So we decided to leave him. I asked Carolina how she got out of Nassau and into Miami? Carolina showed me her new adoption papers that came with an application for US citizenship. Wendy Michelle already having my last name had both a Bahamian and US passport. Wendy Michelle and Carolina told the immigration they were sisters coming to visit their father. Carolina did have her Bahamian passport and was also written in on Wendy Michelle's passport. With that taken care of, I asked if they were both in love with Malcolm. Lori looked at me and said don't you dare. Lori knew what I was thinking. I then asked them how their being here would help Malcolm decide. Wendy Michelle said they had decided that Malcolm would have to come for one of them and the other would stay here. I looked at Lori and she raised her eyebrows. I then asked if Malcolm knew they were here; the girls said they had told Malcolm this morning that if he wanted one of them, he should come for her, but only one.

I then called June and talked from my room with the door shut. I then called my Nassau attorney and asked him get someone to do the leg and paper work so the two girls could start school here.

I then called Lori into the bedroom and asked what would harm them sharing Malcolm. Lori said neither girl was pregnant. Lori said that one girl should be enough and I shouldn't accept my girls to be shared by any man. Malcolm, she said, should be happy with either girl, but if he doesn't show, Lori said there would be a line of boys from her school smiling from ear to ear. So she asked, Can the girls stay? I said that they weren't to miss school and no boys unless I approved first.

I was expecting a call from Malcolm, but he didn't call. I thought about it, and I agreed with Malcolm that if I were him, it would be hard to choose one. It was like Michelle and Deanna back in those days, if Michelle wouldn't have been Bob's girl and she wouldn't have been working her men angle, which one would I have chosen? Hell how long did I ever last with just one girl?

I again called June and let her know what was going on with the girls.

June said that she loved seeing Kayla playing with the other children and both were happy there. She said it would be nice if we all had the same last name.

That night Fernando called, Maria was quite up-set at the news about the accident. Maria had become quite close to Christina. Maria would go to Paxi to assist with training, while Fernando returned to the Jungles of southwest Nicaragua. Fernando's mission was to find how the Beast could have kept its laser charged.

This mission was to be kept as secret as possible. I had already had been asked about the Beast's possible weapon, and there was a good possibility that one of those men that the Beast was chasing that had run by us could have survived and told the story of the Beast and its weapon.

It was Lori's first time meeting Carolina, Carolina was a pretty girl that had just turned 15, Wendy Michelle on the other hand was 16 but looked much older. I thought about how Lori would take the girls walking around the apartment in their nighties. Heck I wondered how I was going to take it.

We had dinner in and at least for Lori it was a school night. Lori thanked me for helping the girls, after all she said, she was their step mother. You might not be so happy once you've seen Carolina in a bathing suit I said.

Lori asked if I was ready for my hot shower? I said I thought she would never ask.

The next morning I was informed by Jack that the ground lasers at Paix were in place and ready for action. Jack was ready to return to the coast of Columbia but I asked, instead that they give support to Fernando. By support, I meant that Jack could use TESS's heat scan and any satellites that passed overhead to assist Fernando's group. TESS would also be able to detect any ground movements.

It was late afternoon while at Lori's swim practice that my cell rang with the news that I needed to get to my computer. Wendy Michelle and Carolina were with me at Lori's practice and I left them to come back with Lori. I raced back to the apartment and got to the computer.

Jack had located Fernando but also two other ground groups. Fernando had already detected the smaller group of just 4, in fact, they had communicated with Fernando notifying him that although they were armed, they were not a part of any military group. They were looking for the same thing that Fernando was. This group were Israelis, they said they were scientists from that same country. I was sure that all Israelis served the same master, maybe not at the moment, but their paths would have had them serving in the Israeli military. Jack noted that the second group was a much larger group of what he said were Cubans soldiers. TESS had identified the Cubans by their speech. Fernando only had seven men plus himself and even with the two lasers they were carrying, they were no match for the 50 or so Cubans. The Cubans were aware of Fernando's group and our C-130. I thought déjà vu and was expecting to see the next message saying that a MiG or two were on the way.

Instead, Jack reported that the Cubans had made a line with two men every ten meters and were moving toward our group. Jack had warned Fernando and Fernando had joined with the Israelis and formed a small protective circle. That was all the information I had at the time.

An hour had passed before I got the next message. Jack had the GPS location of Fernando and had targeted a radius of 100 meters from outside of Fernando and his men. As the Cubans began to rush our group. Jack who had situated the aircraft to pass the Cubans on his port side, had

TESS's infrared locked in on the moving Cubans. As the C-130 flew by, TESS fired the 50 mm rapid-fire cannon. What the cannon didn't take care of, TESS showered them with its lasers. The C-130 then circled back in front of the retreating Cubans but TESS did not cut them down. Jack noted that the computer reported the threat had diminished. Fernando had reported that they had not suffered any loses and that he had taken control of the Israel's radio. Fernando said they would camp together tonight and when daylight came give them back the radio and let them go on their way. Jack would circle around until just after dark then make a run to Honduras for refueling. It looked over, for at least the night.

By now the girls had shown up at the apartment, Lori invited them to the sailing club to see her Morgan. Before they left Bob called wanting to urgently meet. Bob said he would meet me in 30 minutes at the 25 the road Synagogue with a few friends. The girls were on there way to the sailing club, Lori came and asked me to join them, but I said maybe later.

At the Synagogue I met Bob and two other men. The two men looked and smelled like Mossad. They appeared to be alone while I, somewhere was supposed to have three men close by. Bob said the men wanted to talk in privet, Bob excused himself walking back to his Mercedes. The two men introduced themselves as friends of Liz. I told them that being friends with Liz plus a dollar could buy them a cup of coffee. They both understood and smiled. The one looked at me, then said how about Montibelli? I said $.25 cents for the coffee. Then the other man said Carson, I was a friend of Carson he said. We worked in Angola together until we were pulled out. Carson stayed against his orders, the man said. You, the man said, went to his rescue and while in the process sabotaged two of the Soviet's transport aircraft. One made it back to the air strip landing safely while the other had turned back but fell in the rough seas about a half mile short of the air strip killing all 140 or so aboard. You the man said have been responsible for killing more Russians and or Cubans and taking down more of their aircraft than the Entire U.S. military.

I asked what they wanted? A trade they said. You want to return the part you stole for what I asked? They hesitated, then said, we want you to share the technology with us.

I said that would amount to treason. The man that said he was a friend of Carson's said they had something else he said, a third Vehicle. I paused and then said that we would soon also find it. The man said we would not. What are your people looking for at the site I asked? They are searching for the Beast's remains he said. You are looking for the keys I then said. Yes the man said. He then said they believed that the two beings had fought a battle there, both lost a craft. The beast as you called it he said, survived the crash of its craft. We will soon find the craft, we are close I said. We have placed a device that will not permit it to be useful if found they said. We are concerned that the Soviets would locate it. The Soviets are becoming desperate, they will stop at nothing to get a balance of power that they feel they have lost. Still I said, they'd need to deal with the U.S. Government not me. The man was straight forward, your President's health is failing. The Vice President is now setting up for what will be the activation of the war machine. The man said that the Vice President and his group of business men had first started this move with the removal of Kennedy. Johnson was a puppet President he said. The man looked at me and said that I of all people, knew this to be true. Carson knew he said, Carson knew. I said that I would do some thinking, but that I wouldn't stop looking for the other Vehicle as I called it. I then said that they could call off their search for the keys as I put it. The Beast, I said when killed, along with its head, had been relieved of everything it had including the keys.

Bob was signaled to return and Bob said he would drop them off at their hotel and would want to meet me somewhere. I said I'd see him at the Sailing Club.

When I arrived at the club Lori and the girls had just returned from visiting the Morgan. Lori said they would order one of those hoagies and a coke from the bar. Lori and the girls went around to the bar's window while I stepped into the bar. Paul was there and noticed Lori and the girls before he did me. I couldn't blame him, the girls were a site to see. Paul attended Lori and then I caught his eye and Paul said he should have known. The girls took their food out to the outside tables as Bob walked in. Bob didn't recognize Wendy Michelle, Wendy Michelle wasn't at the funeral that Bob had just attended.

Bob and I grabbed a beer and headed out to the dock. Bob asked if I had eyes on? I answered yes. Bob, walking passed the girls said hello to Lori. Lori stood and introduced the girls to Bob. Lori told Bob that both girls were my daughters. Bob said that the time had just passed by so fast.

Lori asked Bob what I was like when he first met me. Bob laughed and said I was a 15 year old boy in search of adventure. Bob then looked my way and back to her saying only the age had changed.

At the end of the dock, Bob asked what the Israelis wanted? I said that he knew darn well what they wanted. I then said that by now at least the Director knew of our meeting and what they were after. Well Bob asked, are you going to help them? Bob said if they couldn't get it one way, they would use other ways. I told Bob that I was sympathetic with their cause but I would not align myself with them or any other group.

Bob said he had gotten the word that the Government would start negotiations with G.D. for two or three TESS units. That's good news I said, they are foolish and didn't hear what I had to say about the dangers. What's the good part Bob asked? Well the good part is that now they can start paying for the advancements and I'll be getting some of my money back. They should be putting their money into the Star Wars project I said. Maybe when they get a closer look at the Vehicle, they may change their minds. Bob then asked if I had taken a good look at the Beast's head before taking it to the Pentagon. I said that I didn't get a good look and by the time I did take any notice it was already too late to have kept it.

Bob then said it was human, a species called Homo Neandertalensis. Bob said that they were here on Earth some 130,000 years ago. Bob continued with him telling a story that some 60,000 years back many of them were hunted and killed taking only their heads. The heads were nowhere to be found. Back then, Bob noted that there wasn't something around that could have hunted them down. Bob paused, then said 20,000 years ago they just disappeared off the face of the earth. Their thinking what I'm thinking I asked. Luckily, Bob said, it was Liz that took the lead on the interest. Liz wants the rest of the body. The scull, Bob said, as you must have noticed has a metal-cased implant.

I was in too much of a hurry to get up there with the head, I was worried about how much trouble we had caused by knocking down those Israeli fighters. I didn't notice the metal plate on its head until I dumped it out on the Pentagon floor. Bob said that I had told the group at the Pentagon that we had buried the body. Liz wants it before this gets to the Vice President. Bob said that them moving the Vehicles to Homestead will take you out of their control.

I asked if he had heard that they would close the Air Force base there? Bob said yes, close one base and open another. In the closing of the conversation, I told him to tell the Israelis no deal.

When I looked, the girls had gone, I went back by to see Paul and ask how Penny and their new born were doing. Paul said all was good with the family. Paul mentioned that June's father that didn't visit the club very often, came by and asked if he had seen me lately. Paul said June's father wasn't too happy that June up and took their granddaughter and moved to Nassau. Paul said that was how he heard the news about the accident. I know that is a big loss to you Jim he said. Please let Penny and myself know if we can help with anything.

Here I was by myself on a Friday night. When I got home Lori was watching TV with the girls. Again I didn't get that kiss when I got home. Once in my room I thought about going by the 1800 club but thought for sure I would get into trouble. Trouble like not coming home trouble. I called Tommy's copilot and asked him to give me a ride. I then just walked out the door leaving a note on the bathroom mirror that said, "gone fishing". I had driven to Opa-locka and had beaten the co-pilot whom was going to fly me to Nassau. I was actually looking forward to a good shower with June and holding her all night. I was still sitting in my car when Eric drove up. We walked to the Leer together, he was on a walk around the Leer and me in the co-pilot's seat when she came aboard. It was Lori, she came to me and sat right down in my lap. Where you off to Captain she asked? I said that I was going to visit and old friend. Male or female Lori asked. Female I said. Lori then hugged me and said that she was sorry about ignoring me. She said she was so excited that she may have made contact with the girls. We are family not competitors she said. Both girls said that they wanted to go to school here, Wendy Michelle, Lori said even wants to try out for the swim team. At this point Eric came aboard and said we were ready. Please she said, don't go. I said that I had heard that she had invited the girls for a sail tomorrow coming back on Sunday. I'll return Sunday afternoon, I said. Lori stood and turned and walked to the Leer's door, looking back with tears rolling down her cheeks said that she would never make this mistake again, she loved me and would be waiting at home for my safe return. Lori then walked down the the steps and slowly headed to the parking lot. I looked at Eric and said that I had changed my mind, stood and walked down the steps and let out a loud whistle. Lori heard the whistle and came a running.

Lori said I was right with what I had done, she said she didn't even notice me leave the apartment. She said she went to use the bathroom and saw the note and went running to catch me. Lori not even returning to the apartment nor telling security, jumped in a waiting taxi not having her cell phone nor the money to pay the taxi.

Lori said that the girls had said that June was beautiful and treated them good. The girls said that June was now getting up early and running on the beach. Lori said that June was getting into shape to get and hold my attention.

I told Lori that I had already seen June in a bathing suit and that for an older woman June, looked pretty darn good. It's not the looking that I'm worried about Lori said. I said that I was having sex with June way before she was even born. Lori said the thought of that wasn't very comforting. Lori said she would cancel that sailing trip for tomorrow. I said I wouldn't miss it for the world. We arrived to the apartment and I received a good hot shower.

The girls and myself would go sailing for the weekend. Jack was still providing cover and helping Fernando search for a third vehicle. While sailing the thought crossed my mine about the river that was only miles from the area that we had killed the Beast. It hit me, if the Beast's Vehicle had some of the same designs, if not flying, it could only charge its system if it were in the water. Yes the Vehicle must be in the river. I used the ship to shore and called Lourdes to have a chopper come and pick me up. Security was given the word that I would be leaving. The girls would get their time alone.

CHAPTER XIV

THE THIRD VEHICLE

Once back at the apartment I sent the coded message about the my thought of the river being where the third Vehicle could be hiding. Locating the Vehicle should be relatively easy to find. It should be just south of where we had encountered the Beast, and there would be no villages on ether side of the river.

I sent the location message via computer with the strong warning that the Israelis should be close by and that they had said the Vehicle was boo-be trapped. I also warned that there also could be, and to stay clear of U.S. Forces that could be looking for the remains of the Beast.

I was somewhat puzzled why TESS hadn't picked up something, I was sure it was in TESS's range. Then I thought we hadn't spent enough time looking at the Beast's body before we had turned it over to G.D. I would contact G.D. To hear if they found anything that might assist in our hunt and add the information that Bob had given up. G.D's return message was that I should come at once.

I was on my way to G.D. when I heard back from Jack. Fernando had split up his men walking the river bank. They had found an over grown trail that came from within the river that looked to head north. Fernando thought this was it but still, having Jack fly overhead TESS found nothing. Jack said he felt if down there, TESS should have found something, but it had not.

Fernando and group would bed down for the night while Jack would fly back to Andros and retrieve Dan, two more divers and their gear plus another 10 men. My reply was that everything was on hold until my return.

At G.D. I was rushed into a lab where their people had taken the Beast's body and explored the body and its DNA. The DNA confirmed the remains as Human. Their guess was that the DNA dated back some 130,000 years ago. What had been surgically added had made the Beast what G.D. thought was a flesh and bone-robot capable of reproduction. Although the head and most of the neck were missing, it had been generically engineered with gills ensuring that this thing could breathe underwater. G.D. stated that without the head with the transplanted brain or controller, what we have is of great value however they thought we should somehow get the head into their lab.

This would take some thinking on my part as Liz knowing what she now knew about the Beast, she wasn't about to hand over her part. We'd better do something quickly as I felt that secrets among their group would eventually reach the Vice President.

With this new information, I was headed to Andros to join Dan and his group. I would stop by Miami to visit my safe and take with me the things that we had stripped from the Beast's dead body. Jack was now on his way to Andros to pick us up. This time the mirror said "Really, I have gone fishing, love you and the baby". Jerry was called and was to have one of our C-130 that was equipped with our first generation TESS units to get in the air in case we needed more men from our southeast base in Nicaragua. Being so close to the boarder, we were not expecting trouble. Once loaded and aboard, the men openly joked who would stand behind me and give me that extra push, off the ramp. This would be my second jump, both at night.

When the time came Jack was standing right there with me but again, we needed Jack aboard. Jack had already talked to Dan about watching over me. There were 14 of us jumping. Dan was expecting us and our gear. Again, stepping off that ramp was like no other experience. This time unlike two months before, the night was clear, I could see the stars and several spots of lights all around but not where we would be landing. On my left I could just make out the river. Then it was the tree tops again. This time I seamed to drop right through the trees, stopping just feet before touching the ground. At least it wasn't raining.

I got myself loose and dropped to the ground. It was great for my feet to hit solid ground. We were dropped from the east moving westerly. The last man to jump waited until we reached him. We were all good to go, no broken bones. We hiked west with each man carrying some piece of diving gear. We met with Fernando's easterly guard. We were then brought into camp and rested until day break.

I didn't think much of the Israelis boast that they had found the third Vehicle, I thought if they had found it they would be busy bringing it up. Boo-be traps, yes perhaps, but left by the Beast.

As the sun came up looking at the terrain we sent two men to follow the trail to get some since it was that of the Beast. We had only two men that could speak some Spanish; we sent four men to the south side of the river, two going east and two going west. Both groups had one man that could communicate with the locals. This was to inquire if the locals had experienced anything strange in the past years with the river or their animals. Jack made radio contact, nothing out of the ordinary. By 9:00 a.m. All three groups had returned each with their reports. The trackers said that the trail was not used by the locals or animals as there were no new tracks. What they had found were trails going off to the west and east almost to the compass. The men sent to check with the locals said that no one lived along the river for a two mile stretch either way. The people were told by family members to stay away from that area. One farmer said that he had given up on raising any live stock as something would carry them off.

This information was enough for me to consider a few dives. Dan and his two men got ready and went in the river at our camp site. Thus far we hadn't seen any boat traffic, the river was more than 50 meters wide at this point. Dan and his men went across and back seeing nothing. Dan then used a sounding pole and started testing the rivers bottom. It was three p.m. and the divers were on their third and last tanks when Dan came up looking excited. They had found something, something much larger than the first two Vehicles. A small marker was placed and the divers returned to the shore line. Dan said they had found a dome that looked like the hatch of a fighter jet but it was almost round shape.

I had time to think about it but still hadn't made up my mind. I had Dan send the two divers back to remove the marker. We pulled up camp leaving three men to stay put with a radio, they were to stay out of sight. We then moved to the center of the cross path that it seemed the Beast had marked. Nine of the group to include Fernando would sleep here without lighting a fire. Myself and another man hiked to the nearest village to the southeast and purchased a ride down the river to were we were dropped off just to the south of our landing strip. Evette had been contacted and Richard was sent in to pick me up and take me to Limon. Tommy would pick me up from Limon and Fly me to Miami. Jack was to make three daily flights up and down the river not to have one of our fiends picking up a pattern.

Once in Miami arriving at the apartment, I realized that it was Tuesday morning and the house woman said that my wife and my two daughters had all gone to school. There was a note on the mirror that Roy had got the girls into school and today Wendy Michelle would try out for the swim team. I noted on the mirror that this was great, I loved her and I was off to Washington and should be back tomorrow. I relocked the Beast's things back in the safe and called Lourdes to see if she had reached the First Lady.

Lourdes said the the First Lady would receive me for dinner with the President that evening. I would have to move quickly. If I went by myself it wouldn't have looked like a social visit. I called June and invited her to Dinner, Tommy would pick her up in an hour and she was to Look like a million. By 3 P.M., June was to have used whatever clothes or jewelry of Salinas' she wanted, and if she needed to buy something in Miami, so be it, but she would need to be at the Opa-Locka airport by 4 p.m. Dinner with the President would be at 8:00 p.m.

I didn't know the President's state of health but I felt with the First Lady's influence I could get accomplished what I had decided to do.

June showed up on time at the airport, she looked like I had never seen her, I thought if she had looked like this 20 years ago things might have ended differently. She looked great. Once aboard I told her where we were off to. We're having dinner with the President of the United States she asked.

The cabin door was open and I could hear Tommy chuckle at June's loud remark.

We were right on time, I had to admit we were a good looking couple. I checked in my arms, this time bringing a small brief case that I put the

the two guns in personally and leaving it giving my usual warning. Beware of the rat trap.

June and I were escorted to the Presidents living quarters and into the dining room. We were greeted by the First Lady. I introduced her to June, June I said was one of my oldest friends and could be trusted.

The President then came in and again I introduced June and the President. The President was quick to asked the purpose of the visit. I was direct and was hoping that he could follow what I was saying.

I first told him that the Vice Presidents wasn't a believer in his Star Wars program. The President then said that the Vice President already thinks he's President. The President said that he would have the entire project funded before he left office. Now he asked, what's on your mind? I asked if he was aware of the second Vehicle and the cost in which we had defended it. Yes, yes he said there were Soviet and Israeli casualties were there not? Yes sir I said. Have you done anything with the second Vehicle as yet he asked? No sir I answered. I then said that I believed that there had been a previous battle fought on the site where that second Vehicle had been found. I believed that the Beast or its group had brought down the second Vehicle that had been retrieved. It has significant damage that is so far unknown whether caused by a tactical hit or the crash it suffered. I then said that we had located a third Vehicle. Does the Vice President know as yet he asked? No one knows I said, but in order to recover it, we wouldn't be able to keep it a secret. I informed him of my visit by the Israelis. The President said he wished he could trust them, but he could not. The President asked how much longer I figured the Sandinistas could hold out? I told him that the soviets were about done in Afghanistan. You mean defeated, he said. Yes sir. The Soviets have almost stopped their oil shipments to Cuba and have drawn down there forces there. If they don't come up with the technology and money soon to keep up with your spending, I believe they will have to retreat on all fronts. To answer your question about Managua, I think one hard push would bring them to a special election. I said I thought Ortega and his group would do better to step back and wait. Wait the President asked? What for? Before the war I said, Nicaragua was a Banana republic, at present they don't even produce bananas. If they once again do become productive, it will take years for the fruit companies to go back. I see no economic gains for Nicaragua unless some outside country came in for some kind of gain. The Communist gain was a foot hold and expansion. I figure it will take 20 years to get back where they were. Ortega will have to wait I said.

The Cubans without a backer will be to busy controlling their Island, they too will have to wait until the times change.

The President asked what my plan was? I said I was looking for some help. Money he asked? No sir, balance, I said. I said that we were ordered to move the first two Vehicles to Homestead, Florida. Once they are there, the Vice President will take them over. He has ordered two TESS units from G.D. TESS as I once explained to you sir is not yet ready. I wasn't worried so much about the first Vehicle because of the computers failure. The Israelis stole a small part and their replacement part failed due to a overload. The Vehicle's computer was burned, G.D. was able to rebuild the computer but, we believe the first Vehicle is now limited. Should the second Vehicle's computer be intact we may have a full operational war machine. The third Vehicle could provide some balance of power. Who the President asked? The Brits I said. The Brits share the base on Andros. If the third Vehicle was moved to Andros under the British flag, we could just strike that balance. Captain the President said, you will be walking a fine line here. Some could see this as betraying your country. Yes sir I said, I will need your get-out-of-jail card. It wasn't the moment to ask for another favor so the Beast's head would either have to wait or I'd look for another route.

Dinner was served and we talked openly about his health. He said that the First Lady was taking good care of him. The First Lady apologized about the President not knowing about my losses the month before. June the First Lady asked? You will assume the roll of wife and mother. June said she had already moved in with the children and was waiting for the other. The President said it would be sooner than later. I stepped on June's toe as I knew she wanted to add that she had been waiting over 20 years. June did not say what she would have liked to.

In the end the President asked if I had a contact with the British? I said that I did. How high up do they go he asked? Right to the Iron Lady I said. The President said he would sleep on it and that if he agreed, I would shortly be contacted by whomever it was from Brits that I knew. The President said that person would get me the word. The word he said was Morpheus, I figured that he was going to say Cowboy. The President said the get out of jail card would only be good while he was still President.

June and I enjoyed the rest of the evening with June telling the story of how we had met while she was washing cars. June said her father still didn't like me but that could still change. June was of course talking about the possibility of marriage.

It was after midnight when we left the White House, I told June, I didn't know how the President could stay up so late.

On the flight back June asked me if I was indeed going to marry her? I told her that I would marry her tonight if I wasn't worried about Lori. But you will marry me this time she asked? Yes I said when the time is right we will marry. Please she said, please do it before someone kills you. Point taken I said.

Tommy landed us in Nassau and we were driven to the first beach house. The house was empty with only a single guard that was sound asleep. Look alive; I said as we walked around to the seaside porch and back door. The door was opened, and I swooped June up and carried her in and into the bedroom. This is the best I can do for now I said. June said for now it was good enough.

The next morning I was up and off early. The house now had at least 4 more guards and I felt safe leaving June sleeping. She had only been in bed for two hours maybe having an hour sleep so far. I had the driver stop at Angee's for some good Bahamian fixens. Ms. Angee was happy to see me and asked about Ms. Lori and Ms. June. We's need to find you a nice Bahamian girl to settle down with she said and laughed. Angee would soon be a grandmother again and said it wouldn't be long before I too had grandchildren. Not so fast I said. Angee said the writing was already on the wall.

Tommy would be waiting to fly me back to Miami. While the flight only lasted less than an hour, there were several messages that had come in and were still coming in.

Omni Tim had sent a message that the first Vehicle was somehow communicating with the second Vehicle. Tim's message said it was just numbers and numbers and they were all in Latin and they had no idea as yet what this meant, but the two Vehicles were definitely communicating.

Jerry had sent in a message asking about if I still wanted the bird on standby for more troops.

Montibelli had called Lourdes asking for a meeting.

Jack's message stated all was good.

And then there was a message from Lourdes that said that our old friend Joe had called. His message said he was on the way to where? I sent a message back to Lourdes and said for him to fly into Miami and to have him picked up and taken to the apartment.

Lee was also looking for a place to stay while in Miami as he would be going back and forth to Nassau from Homestead starting today. I told Lourdes to get a market value on Malcom's house and make him an offer and seal the deal. In the mean time Lee could headquarters in Malcom's house.

Joe on the way meant that the President had called the Iron Lady and made some kind of deal. I wondered when the President slept and then realized the time difference in London could have made a difference.

Before reaching Miami, Lourdes said that Joe was already on his way and would reach Miami by 8:00 p.m. tonight.

I sent word to Bob that I wanted to hire one of the professors that was fluent in Latin and that had NO contact to any government.

By the time I got home the girls had already gone to school. It was a good thing as surely my clothes smelled like June.

I would have lunch with Montibelli, he would again pay me up to date on the Iran transport and inquire about the many stories that were circling of our conflicts with the Israelis and Soviets. I did tell him that two of his Mossad friends had come visit with me. Montibelli said that I should sell them what they wanted. They will pay good he said and in the end the U.S. will share it with them for free. You are too stubborn he said.

Montibelli said that the war between Iraq and Iran would end soon. Both sides, he said are tiring of the war, and we're financially broke. I asked if he would then go into retirement? He asked about me and when I would get out? Montibelli said he would get out when I did. Montibelli mentioned that we both could retire in Nassau.

From lunch I went to Lori's practice. Carolina was in the stands while Wendy Michelle was in the pool. I was glad to see Chubby and the children. The children where getting so big. Both Samuel and Melody came running to see me. Both hugging me not wanting to let go. We all sat together. Lori had introduced Carolina to the family, Chubby and the children knew Wendy Michelle from their Nassau trips.

Both Lori and Wendy Michelle were doing laps. Wendy Michelle had learned to swim before she walked. Wendy had been raised at Michelle's beach house.

Carolina said that Wendy hadn't yet made the team but that the coach said that she was fast enough but the coach needed to see if Wendy would come to every practice and do the required work to assist the team.

This time Lori waited for her break to run and give me my kiss.

From the pool, we all went to the apartment, ate dinner and waited for Joe. I had time to brief Lori that at one time it was the Jim and Joe show, we worked and chased girls together.

Joe arrived down in the lobby at about 9:00 p.m. I went down to greet him and brought him up. Joe didn't know why he was sent and I wasn't sure what to tell him. When the apartment door opened the three girls were there. I told Joe that one was my wife and the others were my daughters. Joe picked Carolina as my wife, we all laughed. Lori introduced herself as my one and only wife. Joe said he didn't get the joke. I said I'd tell him later. Joe and I got caught up, Joe was still single having two x-wives. He had divorced his first wife some 10 years before. At that time Joe rented an apartment for his then-wife, Joe and I had been out partying all night at the 1800 club, we had borrowed a truck and almost from the club went to his house and informed his wife that we were moving her out. Joe's wife said it was hard on her. Joe said it was hard on us too as we were so hungover.

When I sold the port business, Joe was to stay with the group that bought the business, however the Brits that owned a container and shipping business offered him a job. Joe took the Brits job and had been there since. Joe was based out of London, the company that Joe worked for was just one of the cover companies that were run by the British Government.

To get started I went to the safe and opened it up. I pulled out the large canvas like material that wrapped a very old panther's skin. I also took out the photos of the mechanical arm that we found attached to what we thought was a Seminole Chief remains. Also buried with the Chief and still wrapped with the rest was a small laser that we believed was used in preparing the placement of the chief's new arm. The panther skin had drawings that showed several Seminoles fighting a 30 foot crocodile that had one Seminole on the ground and one in the crocodile's mouth. In the drawing, the large croc had a spear in its back. In another drawing there was a small man bending over what we believed to be the Chief. The small man was replacing the arm that the Chief had lost fighting that Croc. I then showed Joe the photo of the crocodile's scull that we had found in the caves. There were also photos of the Croc's broken teeth and the broken cutting tool that matched the broken teeth and interior jaw bone damage. I still had the tool that the Croc had bit off from the machine that had carved the cave's sides. I told Joe that the cutting tool matched the grooves in the side walls of the underwater cave. The two photos that most impressed Joe were the burned hole through the Croc's scull and the large stone spearhead-that had been shoved into and was overgrown by the crocodile's own back bones. Joe's take on what must have happened to the Croc was the same as mine. It was clear that the Croc was not killed by the spear but by the burned hole through its skull. I told Joe that I believed that the drawing on the panther's skin was a written story of what had happened on the day that the Chief had lost his arm by that same Croc. I then told Joe the rest of the story up until before locating the third Vehicle. I then got on the computer and sent a message to Lourdes. Lourdes came back with a message from my old friend Robin. Robin used the code name that the President had said I would receive to move forward with the Brit's.

The first thing I would need was an agreement from the highest level from the Brits. The story would need to go, that the Brits had discovered the location of the third Vehicle and hired me to recover the Vehicle and move it to Andros. There I would would be in charge of the development of whatever information and technology we could find.

The Admiral wasn't going to be to happy, nor the Vice President. With the code name given, I then re-briefed Joe telling him the rest of the story and that they would need the largest lifting helicopter that they could find and I wasn't even sure that would lift the third Vehicle from where it was. The Brits would need one of their few carriers on stand by just off the north west coast of Costa Rica.

Lourdes called and Joe and I were to fly to London for my meeting with the Prime Minister.

It was now past midnight, the girls had gone to sleep. I went in and woke Lori and told her that I would be off for a few days just Joe and I. Lori reminded me that I had a pregnant wife at home and not to get lost or find another young girl working on a fishing wharf.

Joe and I were off to Opa-locks where Tommy would pick us up. We would make two refueling stops on the way, Joe and I had a lot of time to catch up on his life and mine. Joe said he noticed that I was still carrying a gun. I asked if he carried? It was something he said that he rarely did. He noted that by the file they had on me I had made and was still adding to a long list of enemies. Joe asked if I had heard from Karen? I told him, not since Cat had passed away. Joe finally asked about the accident that had killed my Haitian wife and ex-girlfriend. Joe's direct boss Robin had been at Salinas's and my wedding and showed for Salinas's funeral. Joe had been invited to the wedding but said he couldn't make it. Joe said that he had heard it was going to be a surprise wedding. Joe asked how that worked out? Well I said, it was a surprise.

Joe asked about the facility that we were building at Paix and asked if that would continue under the circumstances? I told Joe that nothing had changed with the exception that Haiti would need a new ambassador. Salinas had been pulling double duty. Joe asked if Lori was in that lineup? I said no. I mentioned June to Joe, Joe had never met June. I said I thought that June would step into that role. I mentioned that June had done a good job of mixing with the President and the First Lady at dinner just two nights ago. Joe asked jokingly, you going to marry her too? When I didn't answer, Joe said, oh God. Joe asked about the Sandinistas and how long before they caved in? I told Joe they could drop out at almost anytime. The Soviet's have had it too I said. I told Joe that between Afghanistan, Cuba and Nicaragua, the Soviets had lost a great deal of their tanks, helicopters and a good number of MiGs. I added that their money supplies were running thin. Things started going badly for the Soviet's in Afghanistan when the CIA started providing the rebels there with stingers.

The trip took several hours and once in London, we were met at the airport by Robin. Robin was now living in New York, but had been urgently dispatched back to London. Robin said it was good to see his old friend. Robin had only been briefed of my visit and not why. I was taken straight to 10 Downing Street. There I checked in my arms and was greeted by the Iron Lady herself. I was taken by the hand and lead into one of her offices. Robin and Joe were stopped at that door. The prime minister then formally introduced herself. She admitted she didn't quite understand why I was doing what I was but said that she agreed that I would be in charge of the work but that England would benefit from the technical gains. I explained what TESS was, and my concerns that it wasn't ready to be used without extreme caution. The Iron Lady then handed me a letter that said that the British Government had contracted me to deliver a craft that they claimed the rights of the Vehicle and all of its technology. My new contract did not specify how much I would be paid only that I would share in the profits and technical information 50/50.

She then called in Robin and Joe. Joe was to be their man on the ground. He was to deliver whatever it was to Andros and depending on its size, place it where the first Vehicle was now sitting. Robin was to insure that one of their carriers was on its way to Costa Rica. The British Navy was to be in charge of security.

My meeting was short and nothing like I thought it would be, from this meeting the three of us moved to meet with a British Admiral that wanted to know more about TESS.

The British Admiral asked if TESS and the ground Laser's could be placed aboard a ship.

While visiting with the Admiral I was contacted by Lourdes and was told I needed to get back to the Leer.

Joe understood that something was needing my urgent attention.

Omni Tim had sent word that our engineer aboard the first Vehicle had disconnected the computer from the Vehicle as it seemed that the Vehicle had started going through some kind of systems check list. The Vehicle was locked down so to speak but the engineer aboard said that he though the Vehicle was readying itself to take off?

At present the second Vehicle was in route to Homestead. Thus far no one had even been able to enter the second Vehicle. I feared our chance to do so was gone. The second Vehicle communicating with the first was a mystery. I believed that the possibility of anything being alive in the second Vehicle was nil, however TESS did show that it could think own its own. Wether it had been programmed to do so and was thinking on its own bothered me. The possibility of machines communicating with each other, I believed was real. I then sent a message to Tim asking which Vehicle had sent the first message. Tim came back saying it was the second to the first, then less than 30 minutes later the first sent out what he thought was a reply. Tim then replied that just because we disconnected the computer from the first Vehicle didn't mean that the communications between the the two had stopped. While in the air on our trip back to the states G.D. sent a message that said that our controller that was being studied and was connected to a power source had also shown some unexplained activity. I wrote back the news that Tim had shared.

Joe said that his people could be there with the copter in two days. Again, the only way for Joe and I to be there on site would be to parachute in. Joe being an ex-marine, it wouldn't be his first jump, my third. As it was, again the jump would be at night.

Joe and I stopped in Miami, Lori, along with the girls were home. I got one of my hot showers in which Lori shared the news that Mia was on her way to Miami. She asked, but you already knew this Yes? I said I knew Mia was coming. Lori asked if Malcolm knew. I said he did not. Lori looked at me and asked, get her into school right? I said that I thought that Mia may be heading to Nassau.

The next day I dressed and geared up to include the two card like keys that we had retrieved from the body of the Beast. Joe was sitting on the porch with the girls asking him questions like how long he knew me and where he fit into the picture. The question of him being single also came up. If you remember, Joe was at one time and still was a good looking man. Joe, as Karen use to say was, tall, dark and handsome. The dark part was from always being tan. Joe was an ex-marine whom served in Vietnam, him entering the military just months before I had. Joe did his two years and got out. From that time for ten years it was the Jim and Joe show. As Lori and I walked out on the balcony from our room, we stopped and watched as the girls looked at Joe while they lessened to Joe talk. Lori then turned, hugging me reminded me once again that I had a pregnant wife at home that loved me with all her hart.

Joe noticed us there, finished the story and said he couldn't wait for me all day.

I got my last hugs and kisses for a while and Joe and I were off on the next Great Adventure. We were off to raise a large space craft from the San Jose river.

www.ingramcontent.com/pod-product-compliance
Lightning Source LLC
Chambersburg PA
CBHW031417200726

48285CB00017BA/2419

9781953821676